A Rash Impulse

A Collection of 14 Short Stories: 2020-2022

A Rash Impulse

Your aim must be to take All-Under-Heaven intact. - Sun Tzu

Suspended in the reflection of a child's eye, a minuscule shadow crept up the side of a 1,380 foot building.

Ascending Jinmao Tower, this pupil sized body darkened a small fleck of space against sky-scraping radiance. For a blinking moment in time, an outline of a single man eclipsed all of Shanghai.

This shadow itself felt beady sweat and the eyes of anxious bystanders. He heard the distant percussion of their tongues flapping hundreds of feet below. All the while Han felt protected by a dreamlike facade concealing him.

In spite of his bloodied palms, gnawed at by Jinmao's many layers of upwards stretching teeth, spilled blood was a very small price to pay for his efforts. Perched nestlike between the space of land and air, Han remained entirely unattached to mortality before concepts of consequence lapsed his depth perception. To his own hilarity, he hadn't even taken a thought's notice of the condensed weight of the daily routines he disrupted. It was not an awareness of impending doom nor the blaring of police sirens which suddenly snapped him out of a blur of semi-consciousness, but a white seabird, which oddly contrasted the sky clad pair above a sea of people. To the man, the sight of the seabird contrasting the human ocean made the flying creature seem entirely out of place.

"How strange?" He thought.

Steadily, the thoughts and eyes and minds of onlookers gathered all around the block beneath Century Avenue, a death's leap below Han Qizhi. Besides the casual calls to "Jump!" or to "Get down!" you'd hear at the average suicide attempt, there were a wide variety of macerated opinions blended within the crowd.

Throughout history, many people have performed suicidal stunts for any order of a thousand different reasons. Though several onlookers came to the logical conclusion that if he was not determined to get to the top, he surely would've jumped by now.

"Maybe he's protesting something?" An onlooker wondered.

The onlooker's friend, the spectator responded, "Climbing that high seems like a lot of wasted effort. If I wanted to die protesting something I'd probably just set myself on fire."

The onlooker laughed and responded, "Remember that monk from the Vietnam War or that Tunisian street vendor from the Arab Spring? Now those guys started revolutions."

In rare moments like these people discuss the practicality of self-immolation.

A younger woman wondered out loud, "I bet he's just doing it to be famous. What a desperate attempt that would be!"

Her fiancé, a witty stockbroker, replied, "I've seen a lot of people try to claw their way to the top Shanghai's high society, but not like this."

Other spectators shouted spayed cruelties into thin air or single syllable pleas towards Han's demise. To no avail, he quietly stepped up another several rungs on his concrete ladder.

Han remained meditatively calm. He appeared wraithlike as he mocked the boundaries of the living. A vein of lush sunlight bent off the large window panes, illuminating his body into a flux of rainbows. Many people saw many different things.

From such a distance, dry minds parched of excitement will envision any mirage. Already it was easy to close your eyes and watch him plummet down to reality. They wanted to hear the sound of an ordinary life breaking like glass. They wanted to hear an echo of red lightning cracking the sidewalk at light speed; to see a power washer scrubbing a spontaneous pink mist out of memory. Fame sounded desperate. Protest, certainly wasted effort.

A mendicant and his students witnessed a man without ambition climb the very Pillars of Creation. A baldheaded student asked his teacher why a man would take such a risk and the mendicant responded with a koan.

"If he loves his life he will lose it; if he hates his life in this world, he is going to live here forever."

Of all potential explanations, contradiction is the only apt way to unveil this display of indescribable passion.

An orange clad student remembered the time he saw a male praying mantis' body lurch ecstatically towards his mate and have his doom befall him in one simultaneous swoop. The young monk was sweeping the gates outside of his temple when he witnessed the male mantis's gesture towards fertility. He impregnates the female and she decapitates him in an act of procreation and destruction. Then, she eats him. The student thought it was very strange.

Han continued to climb. The sun had peaked and Jinmao itself seemed like a glass conservatory containing vivid sequins. For a moment Han looked upwards at the boundless sky, and then for the first time at the ground.

In his circumstance, above and below were the same, both leading to a similar form of eternity. An elegant consecration of touch occurred at the boundary between the molecules in Han's palms and in those of the smooth glass windows.

He remembered how he skipped lunch breaks to circle the tower and even dodged work to find the most pristine angles to view Jinmao against the summer sun. True to its namesake, the tower glowed in golden prosperity, changing into an obelisk of pure heat mirrored in sunbeams.

By now the police were assuredly waiting at the top of the skyscraper. Han breathed in. The sea breeze clogged his lungs as the wind harshened height inspired the dizziness of freedom.

The day drew very long; the flickering spires crowning Shanghai set the darkening bay ablaze. Most onlookers who came to watch a suicide realized they wasted their time because Han was almost at the top.

By the last several floors, Han's work clothes were torn to disparate tatters. His hands resembled his clothes. There were red prints that slicked the bottoms of his black soles where he climbed, causing Han to nearly slip on several occasions. His palms were worked down by concrete but he couldn't feel any pain. His obsession marked a discrepancy between everyday decision making and a willpower that mocked an average day's poverty of emotion.

Han's eyes were marked by cold extremity and his senses returned to a silence that empties out ears. His skin was cold from the sky-scraping wind that took him to a place where heart rates raise or lower radically. At such heights there is nothing frivolous about true cold. His brain demanded warm eloquent pulses.

As he climbed, Han craved the heaven infused broth that bubbled as the warm sun settled. Out of a nightmare, storm clouds came in from bayside. He was utterly exhausted and the freshly falling rain water tasted as if it might induce a coma, which would've induced slipping. But Han was meters away from the top of Jinmao's summit and he was moments away from achieving lifelong fantasy.

Against the rain he turned and he saw his life's peak; the pinnacle of his imagination.

As a shoe salesman, he had suffered through years of pathetic, orderly mediocrity. But all that boredom was all about to be smashed. And with the heavy rain came a joyful bliss. He closed his eyes to his favorite memory.

It was exactly a night and a year before his climb.

Evening rain tapped on his kitchen window beckoning him to the roof of his apartment complex. Outside Han saw the lush blossoming of beacons illuminating a world beneath rain drops. His glaze trembled at the thrill of electric blues and liquid sapphires melting into ruby florets. In the distance emeralds flashed in the streets and over tall buildings and inside each wet jewel there contained the polish of innumerable layers of light. Indra's net, which hung over a captive city, was unleashed upon the world.

The rainstorm intensified. The storm was aimed perfectly and the bright nodes of constellations collapsed inwards over Shanghai. The typhoon itself was a perfect catastrophe. Han saw the purity in Jinmao Tower flickering beneath a rain storm of stars exploding over Tianxia.

A display of nature's careless passion swept over the skyline, and he aimed his thoughts at destiny, while the skyline bunkered down against a torrential downpour.

When the morning came, the storm left behind a nebulous mist of smashed stained glass. And still stood Jinmao.

A ladder way illuminated itself in Han's awestruck eyes as he stood atop his apartment building. It was as if Babel itself had withstood the collision of heaven and earth and in the early dawn's vibrance, Han's path was emblazoned on Jinmao's tower side. In exactly one year, he could achieve his life's premonition. It would be wet, but Han would still climb and he would reach the summit.

His eyes opened fully. Han went to pull himself over the final step. As he was about to fulfill his prophesy, the grip of a police officer quickly snagged Han's sweaty dress shirt and pulled him over the side of the spire's railing. The officer was rescuing a man from the edge of history.

After being robbed of his heroic triumph, Han Qizhi was quickly detained by the Shanghai police and imprisoned for a period of two weeks. The official report read that the simple shoe salesman was struck by nothing more than a rash impulse.

More officially, climbing Jinmao Tower became outlawed because the police chief needed to make sure there were no copycat attempts after Han's detainment. While the police chief was genuinely surprised it needed to be said at all, he believed that human beings could not be entrusted with their own dignity.

Though Han's story was mostly forgotten, some memory of his foolish climb lives on. Whether it be somewhere in some Shanghai temple corridors, or in the faint memories of children growing up in well-to-do homes, or in minor articles written many years ago, the story of Han Qizhi still gets passed down almost by accident.

To this day, if you are bold enough and you leap over a barrier erected at the base of Jinmao where Han began his ascent, there might be a tiny placard screwed discretely into a concrete floor reading:

Dedicated to Han Qizhi: A Man of Rash Impulses

Mare Nectaris

When I looked at Carlos Baez I saw an obituary waiting to happen, except that before his flesh fried, it was used as an auxiliary to crime.

That's the fact of the matter and in Lincoln County that meant nothing new to me. In the DoC you can't let these men get the better of you, and that accompanies a fraternizing.

That's how your sense of career ends up undermining job performance. I've had every last insult and every last mixture of human bodily fluids thrown at me, and on many occasions, it has nearly led me to job suspensions.

After many years I got promoted to death row. In my time I've met very guilty minded, fearful men, whose eyes met with terror at the receiving end of impartial justice. Carlos wasn't necessarily one of those sickos who enjoyed what he did, but he certainly had a streak of the *fascination* about him. I've come across people like him in my career too. Regardless, my sole responsibility here was to facilitate their deaths and the due processes accordingly.

One afternoon, exactly two weeks before Baez was set to fry, a visitor came by asking for an interview. He was a writer doing an op-ed for the Times and I told him to come back when he had an appointment. He said he's only in Arkansas for another day and that he had one approved already. Then he asked what else's Baez got to do today?

I asked Baez what else's he got to do today, and Baez just kept looking at the bee hive he was drawing in brown paint on the gray wall. Real wretched smell. Weird freak.

"Mr. Baez seems to be indisposed at the moment, sir."

"With what?"

"It appears to be some sort of artistic endeavor."

"Can I at least get a look at him. Maybe get a picture?"

"No cameras within penitentiary walls mister…"

"Klimt. Can I write things?"

"Well I don't see why not." I said.

***

"Carlos Baez?"

Baez said nothing. He kept staring.

One could imagine that the orange light thrown out of his eyes could've started a fire with a magnifying glass, and besides his terrible eyes his facial features were pinkishly inflamed, and his old jowls were indivisible from his cheeks. Baez had brown-white beard hair up to underneath his sockets.

"Mr. Baez, I'm Bob Klimt. I'm a reporter from the New York Times. I'm here to ask you a couple things if you have the time."

Baez laughed, and then started coughing profusely.

"I got two weeks."

"Two hours will be more than enough time."

"That's not much time."

"It'll be just fine, Mr. Baez."

"That'll be fine for you I mean." He said laughing again.

Klimt pulled a chair up to his cage. He turned to the correctional officer Mr. Dupont, and asked him if they can do a one-on-one interview and Dupont said no.

"Mr. Baez, if I may be bold? I'll say I don't think you killed all those people. And I'll tell you that I'm one of those who agreed that you don't have the self-confidence to be really truly violent with anyone."

"Don't beat around the bush huh? I'll tell you Mr. Klimt. You're right. I ain't a killer at all. Not one for the axe. They got me cuz they found a bloody hatchet in my hand. I was killing chickens, not white ladies. They picked up the first unlucky looking brown son of a bitch they could find."

"Said in the report you were messing around with animals, for pleasure."

"What's the difference between that and killing for sport?" Baez said.

"I think a lot of people would say killing for sport is one thing. You might butcher the game to feed your family. You wanna get it in one shot, so the animal doesn't suffer. But the things you were doing."

"I know what I was doing."

"You were hurting animals for fun. Don't you find that a little unnerving to people?"

"It wasn't for fun. It was for interest. Mr. Dupont put it good. How'd you call it Mr. Dupont? Not fun a?"

"A *fascination*?" Dupont said.

"Yes sir, it was a fascination."

Klimt lit a cigarette and offered Baez one and he took it.

"A fascination." Klimt fixed his spectacles. "And I guess that fascination started with bees?"

"You can say that. I'd call it a bit more of an obsession personally." He put down the lit cigarette on to the metal edge of his cot.

"Here look." Baez pulled out an old cigarette carton from beneath his bed and slid it in between the bars of his cell towards Klimt.

Tenderly, Klimt took the carton and discovered a carefully procured cornucopia of dead insects, mostly hornets and wasps.

They shook around loose, and dried to the standards of an entomologist. Baez kept a particularly beautiful arrangement of beetles.

Klimt admired a beetle's minuscule shell which reflected from its iridescent body the blood-rays of pliant sun. While holding it up to the sunlight Klimt saw how a man set to die by electricity could get lost in a prism of lustrous colors. He placed it gently back amongst the moths, and a yellow butterfly, and wasps, and slid it back through the bars to Baez.

"Is this enough to spill blood over?" Klimt asked, titling his head up back towards the wall painting.

"I'll tell you my fascination with bees began naturally as a result of the harvesting process, from the farm where I was raised. My first interest revolved around the order of a bee's life, how it gave itself over fully to a compulsion to sniff out pollen, and to carry back as much of it as possible for the hive's alchemical purposes."

Klimt showed surprise on his face at the man who was previously assumed to be a completely impulsive idiot.

"I remember the first time I saw bees sting something other than me. It was our dog. How the bee flung itself headlong into a creature much larger than itself. I was obsessed with that."

"Is that why you killed your little cousin?"

"I didn't kill him." He flicked his cigarette outside of the cell, where it landed just short of Klimt's shoes. "It wasn't me who killed him."

"Then what happened?"

"Let me tell you that story by telling you another."

He stood up and walked over to the metal seatless toilet. Baez turned his back to the prison cell bars, unzipped his pants, and started pissing.

"When I was around 9, I was going back outside the apiary shed, just before the meadow, where we stored our raw honey, and my dad told me to go fetch some. Some customers came, somewhere from out east, New Jersey area, and they were driving out to Ohio. When I walked out back, I reached into the shed cupboard and cracked the honey jar open on the desk. I paced over to the door to make sure no one could catch me eating some. And when I turned I saw a little mouse, lurking on the second shelf of the wooden desk, just above the jar."

Baez finished up and flushed and kept telling his story, walking back over to his cot.

"Suddenly falling from the desk's second shelf, I saw the little mouse toss itself into my open jar. At first it was innocent enough. The mouse fumbled in the jar and seconds passed. Then it turned into a disaster."

Baez was looking Klimt cold dead in the eyes.

"The rodent, subdued completely by instinct, realized immediately afterwards that its humanlike fingers could not reach the lip of the jar. Still, he spun around in panicky excitement, nibbling nectar off his paws, sinking deeper down into pleasure. His nails scraped on the jar's glass walls, almost escaping over the top. Then he went back to eating again. The poor creature was writhing between its instincts."

"And what did you do?" Klimt asked.

"I didn't do anything. Watched it. I learned something about the animal instinct. There's no logic to it you know? That day, I saw the two domineering desires which commanded the animal mind, split the creature in two. One voice shrieked upwards in flight, and clawed at me for life. Another instinct demanded a ravenous compliance to eat. The stronger will won out. The one that pulled him downwards to satiate hunger. I stood transfixed by this biological fission erupting between two desires rooted in the same energy. The mouse couldn't even trust its own instincts. Both instructions were telling him the same thing, just in two opposite directions. Just live."

"Did your Pop find you?"

"Never. But I think that day, it wouldn't have changed much if he did, cuz I was a changed boy."

Baez thought back to his childhood bedroom.

A largely vacant one with wooden walls, and a draft in the winter time. He thought about how the seasons passed, and how he felt laying in that bed, looking out the window when evening would come. On bleak midwinter nights, he could remember how his death infatuation was something he had begun to feel an anxiety about. How he could see the way his family and friends at school were looking at him, especially after Andy died. Somehow they knew there was something more than a deadly allergic reaction at hand.

Outside the window, the child Baez shuddered at a feeling of dark transcendence about the world. He'd come inside from sneaking out for early morning walks and think to himself, "In the winter I could live." In his memory, he saw the moon illuminating the earth in constance. The way light reflected into his eyes, reflected the meadow's scarcity, no more fertile than a lunar lava plain.

He also remembered the summer day his cousin died. And told it all to Klimt.

Frankly, he could profess no emotional attachment to his actions. He had to confess a scientific appreciation for spiritual death. It wasn't the decadence that fascinated him. It wasn't the act of cruelty, the killing of small rodents, dropping them in honey jars, watching them writhe. Watching slowly, waiting for the synapses to stop firing, waiting for the green flash to ignite and let the mouse's spirit rip from life's sunset. He believed in religions, and he believed in God. He was terrified to find out the Truth, but needed to test the boundaries, to find out if he could see something, find anything angelic, when a body dies.

"Cousin Andy came for a visit when he was a very little boy. Maybe six, and he escaped the house with me. And we ran down to the meadow in the summertime, when the flowers basked in full fervor. He got stung bad. He's allergic. And I didn't tell anyone, and I didn't say nothing. He just got stung, and boy did he plump up too, and I saw it. I saw something I can't describe. Something religious, I don't like to get too, um, supernatural. But something clicked with me. I knew God was real. And then his momma caught me watching him. And she screamed and he croaked."

Klimt didn't say anything, and even Dupont, in his decades with the Department of Corrections, was horrendously offput.

"But those other people. Those girls. I didn't kill them. I'm not that typa guy. You oughta know that."

Klimt was at a loss.

"Mr. Klimt, I have a real fascination with the winter. You can catch a glimpse of the osmosis of life. Feel the air in here. In this cell. The mistral air measuring the width of our lungs, dictating the cost of our breathing, the cost of diffusing heat."

"And you expect me to believe you're not a murderer?"

"I ain't one. I ain't a bad guy. I just have fascinations."

Klimt didn't want to do this interview anymore. Maybe he wasn't cut out for it, so he got his papers, picked up the folding chair and nodded his head at Dupont.

"Mr. Klimt, you look like you're just about wrapped up here. But before you get up I gotta tell you something. You see that moon coming up? You see them stars too huh? Right out my little window. I'll tell you what, my younger cousin felt as far away to me as all these things. At night, during the winter, I could imagine to myself that he'd been buried in a black space out there between the star fields. It made no difference to me if he had sunken beneath the Mare Nectaris, or under some soil one hundred feet away from my bedroom."

Air vapor blew out of Baez's mouth as he was talking, walking over to the window.

"To me, Andy is a shade blemishing the moon. That's all he is to me. When Andy died I learned that I could be as spiteful as I wanted towards King

Death because he would never make any sense. There made no difference to me whether Andy was out there, buried meagerly beneath a bed of flowers, or washed away down the Milky Way. He could be buried under this jailyard for all I care and I would sleep, and I will continue to sleep and will sleep well, for the rest of my rotting body's one thousand days."

"You know I can't wait to write your obituary."

"I look forward to it."

"One more thing Baez. I did my research on you. You look a lot like him. Your cousin."

Klimt was guided out by Dupont.

That was the last of it. The time came. No clemency was asked. No last minute Hail Marys. Just the chair. And the electricity and execution and then an obituary.

As a matter of fact, Klimt drove all the way back down two weeks later to fill a seat as a witness to the execution. There were several people sitting in attendance. A young lawyer sat down next to Klimt. The man was from Baez's defense team. Klimt and Vince Newell shook hands and introduced themselves to one other. Newell said he read Klimt's article. Then Newell said Baez told him the honey jars are still out there. He said they're buried behind a storage shed out at Baez Farm.

A year to the day after Carlos Baez was put to death in the state of Arkansas for triple homicide, Klimt made the pilgrimage back down to Lincoln County. In the early evening, he parked his Buick on an overgrown path where the driveway should've been. Klimt got out and walked around back, past the decrepit home and made it to the shed. It was overlooking a terribly overgrown array of flowers, barely a meadow now, where he turned his head to see a window built into the rotten wooden home. It was small, like a bedroom window.

After digging around for a while Klimt took a break to look at the yard, and the boyhood farm of the murderer Carlos Baez. Klimt looked towards an old farm field where the apiary would've been.

He saw the overgrown meadow contrasting the sky, hanging its possessions vibrantly above frozen lilies in the nudity of their dying stage. The Mare Nectaris, accentuated at twilight by an Indra's net of burning pearls.

"If I was Buzz Aldrin or Neil Armstrong I would've almost certainly gone awol up there." Klimt thought out loud. And then he nicked something and dusted the soil off, and in the moonlight he held a relic of a minor cataclysm, mice and rats stuck in decrepit angles, some red-eyed.

In the jar, in the abyssal redness, an experiment held its victims in frozen honey. Klimt began to figure that there are some relics, some pieces of the past, which command a talisman of darkness. Maybe Baez didn't kill those people, maybe he did. That was there and then. What Klimt held in his hands right now was material evidence of empirical evil. Was that true? The question of the thought was answered in his head by a renunciation his previous morals. There is a transcendental darkness on planet earth that says there is room to spare on this graveyard moving through space time. Klimt couldn't figure it out, but something meditatively evil was laid in a ditch before him. Who is to say that such meditations on cruelty cannot also be encapsulated in a koan describing pure malevolence as a singularity? Not unlike the Shroud of Turin, or a golden reliquary box containing a finger bone of Gautama, there could be objects in this realm that detail a vortex of transcendental suffering. This jar of honey, this jar of mice, was one such artifact.

He placed the glass jar of mice back into the dirt. He couldn't think to carry it with him, or to destroy it, so he covered it up in the soil. Honey and glass decay very slowly. Though Klimt knew that one day, more than likely, he would have to return to the scene of this travesty and destroy it. Klimt figured, in a not so decisive way, that the world was filled with little treasures of undiscovered horror.

He also felt that the human race would be reduced as a whole if the knowledge of this evil in the world was unveiled. It would have to be hidden.

Klimt, in his old age, would return to haunt the scene of the crime many decades later. He would dig down into the earth to find the little jar of mice, dead and serene.

And many more years later, he found it missing.

Cage Fighting

"The truth is I've tried and failed at so many things that it happened almost by accident."

We sat together on a pair of folding chairs watching TV, looking at the fight replays, while my subject was watching himself beat the piss out of his opponent on a national broadcast. He smelled sweaty, and resembled a culmination of his vicious talent. The 25-year-old Thomas Burzinski had just won his second UFC bout by TKO in the 56th second of the first round. He was my age.

Thomas continued, "It's not for the money. God knows we aren't compensated well after our hospital bills are paid. And privately I don't have the sort of bloodlust my fanbase would like to imagine I do."

My eyebrows furled inwards in disbelief. "You licked your gloves after the fight ended."

"I did, but that's just a selling point of my style. I'm like a circus clown in that aspect. Still, every performer takes the mask off and goes home at the end of a show."

"A circus clown that smashes orbital bones? And enjoys it?"

"I suppose when you put it like that then yes." He paused to swish his gums with a drink of water, then spat bloody water onto the ground. "But let me ask you, what if I like it? And let's not beat around the bush, people do enjoy it. Spectators and combatants alike."

"It packs the arena."

"I have no doubt in my mind that if this was a fight to the death, these bouts would sell. Hell, maybe even more so. I'd hate to think we've made so much moral progress since the days of the coliseum. Now wouldn't such an ancient spectacle be a waste today?"

Thomas's face looked like it was smashed by a tire iron. It was too swollen to make detailed expressions.

"That sounds very vulgar."

"Oh fuck off. You sound like a menopausal professor."

"I… Uh. I don't mean that in a critical sense. Even the Greatest, ended up with severe Parkinson's from getting hit too much."

"Let me provide you with some insight about the way I feel about it from my first professional fight. As I was limping out of the cage, little rings of smoke popped up around my dry heaving head. I'd moved so much, so fast, in the octagon that I might as well have breached the sound barrier or survived a grenade explosion. And while the man opposite me lay breach in defeat, I stood tall and exited the cage on my own, birthing myself, finding a new life. The crowd's cheering was muffled by my carnage clogged ears. But I'll tell you nothing compares to the feeling of escaping combat alive."

"Thomas, when I watch you fight, you seem to get a legitimate delight out of the suffering and I get that. But…"

"But what?"

I couldn't respond.

Thomas continued, "Let's analyze me a little more. In fact let's just cut to the chase. Yes I enjoy the suffering because it makes me feel very alive. It's not sadistic, it's not masochistic. No I don't take any sexual pleasure out of it. So don't bother asking. I'll say this, I take absolutely no issue acting in accordance with the reflexes of nature. Fighting lets me slip back away from this curse called consciousness, and allows me to behave as absolutely wretchedly as God, or whatever nature intended me."

We took a pause to watch one fighter choke out another on the flat screen.

"You want to hear what sickens me the most? The vice of indulging in the apparition that a civilized nature is an ascendant one. That desk jockeying. Feeling the wrath of a machine unimaginably greater than you. Letting it reap hours from our precious few moments. I hate the subdued cowardice involved in negating every impulse. Ignoring the embedded impulse inside that is screaming, begging us to do something completely irrational, something so irrational that it might even make us happy. Christ forbid, we transcend the pathways directing us towards fruitless humiliation."

"Are you talking about me?"

"Do you have to ask? I mean you seem somehow unhappy to be here, interviewing a fighter, and here we were talking about sacrifice and cowardice."

He continued. "If there's one thing I've learned in this profession, it's that everything is a sacrifice. You sacrificed your time to get in the car and drive to Vegas from who cares where and ask me poorly formulated questions. Think about the breath you're wasting." He swished more water and spat. "Sacrifice occurs even at the expense of dreaming."

"Well I…"

"Well what?" He cut me off and began mocking my voice. "Let's imagine another ancient spectacle. Even the great Muhammad Ali ended up with Parkinson's. Doesn't that seem like such a waste? You might as well swim straight out to sea and find out if you really enjoy living if that's your thought process."

"Maybe I have."

"Maybe you didn't swim far enough."

And with that he got up. Before he left the locker room, he turned to me and said, "Everyone will look at you and simply say you can never act irrationally. Of course there has to be a deep seated reason why your random impulses sublimate into delight. It's because I'm good at what I do and it makes living pay off. So fuck you."

He walked out.

A couple minutes later I found that I forgot to turn on my tape recorder.

Several months later, Thomas "Polish Pride" Burzinski stepped into the ring again and tore his Brazilian opposition to shreds. I watched a rerun of the main card from my hotel room in Reno and analyzed the manner in which Burzinski waged war. Steadily, it transformed into an act of daydreaming.

On TV I watched his butterfly feet pop up and down against the pink canvas. He floated around the octagon freely, dancing even. In each jab Burzinski's arms swelled up, tempting a counterpunch. It was precision. He was setting up siege equipment around the octagon.

About a minute in, the combatants began throwing bombs, ending their mere flirtation with violence. The Polish fighter's arms swung twin battering rams, knocking at a weak flank protecting Mora's heart and liver. Mora felt his vitals exposed by his torso's collapsing bastions. Thankfully for Mora, the bell rang, signaling the end of the round.

The two fighters went to their stools and sat down. At one end I could imagine, not just trainers and coaches, but Clausewitz as Burzinski's corner man, assisted by Hannibal feeding the fighter lessons in strategy. 14 seconds into the second round, Thomas's spear knee toppled the citadel. Burzinski flew in for the ground and pound and Mora went to sleep. My eyes were glued to Burzinski, the exemplary MMA practitioner, whose art is to put a succinct stop to life.

That last phrase popped into my head and got the ball rolling so I sat down at my laptop and tried to imagine something he'd say.

It went like this:

"Since my first fight I couldn't stand the feeling of embittered alienation. I hated that. I was the enemy of that. Each day of my life was a war against who I was in comparison to who I could be. Inside the cage, my memories are rehearsed by one another in terms of a suffering staccato. There's nothing smooth, just jittery instances of inflicted pain. I remember how I looked at my opponent. Mora's tan skin was a veil for pale flesh behind a blood-drained face. For a moment I was able to punch outside of myself. I got a ringside view of my own body, stabbing and grappling, demanding to be felt. I looked at my muscular legs, taught like the trunks of a young oak, flexing around a body tightened up by weight cutting.

Then I saw Mora, who chastised the image of the brutalist fighter. His ornate face lunged towards me, heaving its statuesque magnitude. In the second round I fashioned his body out my image. In the cage I was the artist of my opponent's body. I hopped around, poised to mold his condition into vivid, lung bled breaths.

Out of my opponent, I refigured a living statue of the Dying Gaul. My high knee peaked spearlike after a feigned jab, knocking him to his side.

At first I stood stunned, silenced by my accomplishment, then I dove in, ravenous, hawkish, death defiant. My hammer fist smashed against Mora and mercilessly exiled his mind from his body."

As soon as I finished my exalted report, it didn't matter to me whether or not I was performing real journalism. So I sent this bullshit interview to *Victory MMA Magazine*. Sitting deep into my hotel desk chair, I realized what an absolute coward I was.

I slumped sick into my chair, daring not to feel sorry for myself. Slowly tears of self-hatred began to well up in my eyes. No, these tears were tears of fear, of self-preservation. I'll be safe forever. No Parkinson's. No legacy. The only thing happening at my time's expense is the guarantee of doing absolutely nothing. Maybe he's healthy and I'm sick. Maybe I'm the one who deserves the interview, as part of a documentary on pontifical failure. I started to laugh and I started to dream again. I knew at the terminal exchange of life for breath, I'll never have to sacrifice my fantasies. Not even on accident.

Tragicomedy: How To Get Over Yourself

The Influencer is a new archetype. He exists solely as a cultural mile marker on the path to ever increasing atomization.

When our culture finally becomes completely devoid of spirit, people, as empty spiritless husks will blow like tumbleweeds down into the never ending journey inwards.

That endless path inwards is void because there is nothing world-fertile about the spiritless within. Call it less than zero-ness. Without spirit, we will find ourselves evermore exiled to the universe within ourselves. It's meditating without emancipation. After all, somebody said, "Euro-Buddhism is a pitstop to nihilism."

The social alien without connection to the spirit can delve inexorably into the psychological world. (Isn't the mind the widest conceivable horizon?) In a way psychological introspection and endless self-analysis is not unlike the scientific venture towards the infinitesimally small. We discover atoms, then quarks, and certainly smaller subatomic particles. Not unlike units of matter in the world, there are nearly infinite ways to break down the psychological self into smaller and smaller bits; feelings about feelings and thoughts about thoughts. At what point does it become useless? More importantly, does it make us feel any better about anything?

Occasionally the strangeness of our culture is so incomprehensibly weird that you can only laugh. This is because there is something very fertile about laughter. At what point do you become a subculture of your own, a culture of one, underneath your own microscope?

How To Get Over Yourself

Part 1:

It was calm and I was floating nearly naked in the ocean water.

As ropes of water ran across my body like lukewarm sapphires, my eyes dreamed upwards at starry shambles of floating light. And I floated and dreamed on the water, and the sky twinkled; I blinked salt out of my eyes and saw the bountiful night reflecting all around me, perhaps even upon me. It made no difference whether I was a star down here, or up there, at the ocean's surface, we reflected the exact same way.

As lukewarm night, rushed over my head, pushing my hair shorewards, I floated there, in between sleep, in between drowning. Imagine a man simply going to dream in the water forever. Whenever I'd come too close, a strong wave would tilt me gently away from slumbering and gently away from death. When my joints hurt from the toll of running or lifting, I could, at the end of the day, tilt my mind back into the lolling rill of darkness, and alleviate myself from gravity.

Over a steady course of several years I discovered the monumental role that the irrational played in my life.

I'd sit at the computer for instance, and pluck away at copywriting, as though each letter cost me a piece of hair. Plucking, day in and day out, until my scalp had been bared. Even my eyelids were vacant of lashes. All this time, I was hunting for the feeling of freedom in place of happiness, and ignoring the fulfillment of love, in search of art in some vacuum.

I was thinking a lot about who I was, and how I came to be. Thinking consistently about myself, more so than I had in past. Only recently had I thought about how I came to confess a new, modern profession.

The career path of the social media influencer let me dissolve into fantasy. If I am a narcissist, then you (my audience) are the co-conspirators in my identity. I'll say it once right here, and I won't be particularly embarrassed if you like it or not, all of the characters I became uttered forth a bizarre illusion and are totally dependent on the implication that you believe in them.

Despite being a very egotistical person, I have a surprisingly deprecating inner monologue. Among other things, this inner voice was constantly telling me to hurt myself. It took me a while to understand how this internal monologue was offset by a polylogue in my Instagram comment section, that has direct access to a happy button behind my eyes. In essence, there was a jihad going on in my skull; taking place between deep seated self-loathing and emoji heart numbers.

While neither the positive comments I received for my revealing physique posts, or the thoughts inside my head telling me to off myself were exactly limitless; an attritional conflict was still taking place. At some point one antagonist would exhaust, and I felt as though I would be overcome by either vaporous bliss or subliminal annihilation.

As technically unremarkable as the "water splashing with tongue out emoji" is, and as illogical as it is to invest my lifetime into romanticizing my youth online, it is perhaps more irrational to be constantly predisposed to a negatory death obsession. So ultimately, again, I am subjecting myself to the irrational, because he is my familiar, because surrendering myself to chance outcomes in happy hopes are nothing new to me.

As I floated there watching water subsume my toes beneath the waves, I thought that I would have reached a point of stability by 28, to not have to make such absurd claims, even in the fundamental privacy of mind.

The part of me that was not interrupted by intrusive thoughts, and could settle down briefly by the Pacific Ocean side, thought that solace would walk hand in hand with success. Sure I am financially stable. I've amassed a cavalcade of appreciation from fans. I get to go around the world making beautiful content for people, but my blood never cooled.

A flash of lightning burst a couple dozen miles off the shore to the south. The lightning flashed like a script writ orchid-like in the black clouds and I heard the word of lighting enunciated overhead.

Walking back up to the resort apartment rental, a slight rain fell on my skin. The wind took to the palms trees sailing leaves and I picked up my pace. In the warm Hawaiian rain, there was a happiness to be away from home.

In Western Pennsylvania it was very cold right now so it was nice to slouch in the tropical weather. Off the beach and onto the a promenade, I flip-flopped down a concrete path by a gated pool and unlocked the lobby door with a swipe card key.

Crossing my mind on the elevator ride up was a list of the cool shit I had to do tomorrow with the pretty girlfriend/stand-in I paid to appear in my vlogs. Klara Scott was her name.

After getting back into my rental I went to go wash off in the bathroom. Must've been the change of moisture in the air because my nose started bleeding. My knuckles sutured my nostrils and let the blood clot. Blood threads caught at the back of my nose got spit up and got washed down the drain.

After getting out, I began analyzing my image in the mirror, preparing for tomorrow's photo shoot.

At some point I was staring at each individual hair and freckle and pustule on my face. It was a meditative exercise. There is a strategy developed by Buddhist monks, which allowed them to dissect each part and parcel of an object of desire, and reduce it to its core components. This was a dissociative act.

Perched on the porcelain sink, I began leaning in forehead to forehead with a gorilla who's finally met his match. This was a scene from a nature documentary about a primate who's reflection had only recently lost its alien status. That human being in the mirror, might be in some way attached to my body.

Dare I say, he is somehow aligned with my mind. This was a synthesis of body and spirit. Kierkegaard speculated that that's what makes a man. I was looking him dead in the eyes, down into the stark, brown barrows, into the blackness of the pupil's reflection, into a human devoid space, into starkness of pupil upon pupil, daring to think out loud that *he* might be *me*.

There was of course a vacancy of, I suppose what one might call authentic personality, or individuality. In one on one scenarios I was very good at adapting to social environments and utilizing whatever characteristics worked best. It was fun, like acting. Any introspection that carried on was a venture into a hall of mirrors. Inside the mirrors you'd catch a marbling of faces, a swerving elasticity of expressions, or memories attached to different archetypes, but what that hall deflected was of schizoid nuance.

That body of thoughts, of experiences, looking at itself in the bathroom mirror was a catalogue of experimental responses to emotion, was essentially not a human at all but a machine learning to be a man.

It, him, I, became an influencer because I was good at it. The job meant relaying desires. That's all it was. The word alien comes up again. One time I saw a movie about an extraterrestrial spy who assumed the guise of an earthling male, and he was assigned the responsibility of gathering intelligence on the human race. It was like that for me, except in the movie the alien falls in love and blows his cover. For whatever reason that could never happen in reality because I am not alien.

I wouldn't call it sympathy, but I got very good at relating to others. In fact, I was leechlike in my capabilities to drain character traits swimming in the same lake as me. If I felt a sudden despondency brought on by loneliness, or the need to create a certain friction in the flesh, I could lavish into lies to get my way. Sometimes I could cry because I believed everything about the type of man I was. Even the really stupid pathetic shit.

One time I was able to eek out a pitiful emotional reaction the week after Trump got elected at a craft brewery. A beautiful young women swept my tears away with her thumbs.

I told her about the time I volunteered to go down to the Gulf of Mexico and scrub grease off oil stained seagull chicks. Or about the time I almost died in a hunger strike to protest for the liberation imprisoned illegal aliens… I mean refugees. And we were both plastered enough to believe me.

At a barbecue party in Memphis, I told a Black Republican, who happened to be remarkably lovely, that the Democrats are the party of the real racists and that Lincoln helped free her people. She took me back to her apartment that night, and you get the point.

The vaccine is horrible. What do you think? I mean it's horrible that so many people don't get it. Do I think the pandemic is a hoax? Let's get the politics out of Congress, that's what I say. I think they're all crooked. Except Pelosi? I mean Bush? Wait. Don't go.

You win some you lose some. One day I'm a Marxist, the next day, we can talk about my church and the pro-life rallies I helped organize. I really am just a party of one. A man representing his own loneliness. Is it so bad to say? I don't care.

The comedy is that there was no lie that would go untold. There were no boundaries that would go unbreached. My very unusual problem was that my limited experience with love extended to the point where I experience every ecstasy adjacent to a relationship but not affection.

I am brought under a manifold with other people. I understand the ferocity of their touch, the fragrant glory of scent, and the vivacity of the eye, all stemming from human beauty, but an obligation, an attachment to them, is not there.

I've uncovered every inanity of human interaction but not romantic love. I can sense when somebody is not charged with a desire to possess me.

I have a drive to be desired, to become the ideal desire. And the want is so much more intense than the moment of accomplishment. To be wanted is everything. A very dumb way of putting it, but that was an immaculately narcissistic faculty of my career path. Become an object of desire. I wanted to exist in a perfection zone of fantasy, in the borderline space of sexual desire. I wanted to wield the influence of wanting, and if I could not be loved, I would have to raise an awareness of my own desirability.

My jellylikeness of character, driven by this desire of desire, made me as clever as an octopus. And just like an octopus, I can shape myself into any identity shaped hole. I lose traits, regrow lost limbs, and mold into whole new identities. There was a brain operating within this gelatinous organism, but its modus operandi was of no real importance. The spectacle of my motives is attraction enough.

The octopus spreads itself thin. It camouflages. It is united by all of its limbs. Its deceit is a morpheus device of desire. I was so enrapt in this role because I knew one thing: dream is the apex slavemaker. Dream is the apex desire. I fell asleep and woke up the next day.

Part 2:

I met her in the lobby. On a rental scooter we drove together 30 minutes inland from the beachfront.

On our way up the road to the volcano we were giving attention to the lush green mountains. I can recall the way we stepped close to the shores of a lava flow and the way new stone slipped clean onto the black glass banks of a molten river.

After volcano photos, we went for lunch at a poke place and that was good. I enjoyed watching this pretty girl eat. She was skinny. Klara wore a yellow bikini beneath her denim overall shorts and ate with the tuna with decorum. Her chopsticks balanced the red chunks with slivers of sweet onion. I liked the way the ocean water curled up her pretty blonde hair.

Klara was nice. I couldn't think of much more to say about her other than that. It was strange considering how insulting that might be sound to tell someone.

We went for surfing lessons together. It was nice to see her enjoy her time by the coastline. Little silvery fish came up to our feet to eat old skin off our toes. Together, we sat by the shore taking joy in that.

The photographer we hired captured the right bits of one another. Klara was trim, and her muscles were angular. The sun highlighted her skin nicely, and gave the appearance of a exceedingly fit 26 year old woman. She was nice to look at, and be seen by, but not nicer looking than me. As we modeled for more photos, I got a sense of the way people were looking at me on this Oahu beach. It was disdain.

I gave her 300 dollars cash and a handshake and she went back up to her apartment. That was all.

The pictures were well done. They would feed the algorithm.

On the internet I washed my narcissism in a bath of love. The badness in me was re-baptized as one of the best qualities you could have. People loved the dieting advice and they adored the positivity, the plagiarized peacocking, the financial tips. I couldn't realize how much of me was something stolen.

Next month I was going to Ibiza to promote an event at a dance club, so all I could think about was losing weight to maintain my form. And then I began to wonder whether or not I was thinking clearly. In moments of physical exercise, clarity breaks through from the other side. In physical exercise, I had the sensation of shedding excessive thought.

Physicality shed mental weight off my body because running is a prophylactic against mental obesity. After several hours of photo editing, the fine summer's day passed by and the late evening came. People were coming up from the pool or the beach to lay down and around 8 PM, I went past the promenade and my feet hit the sand. The air felt nice.

How I held fond memories of running in the bracing night at my old home in Pittsburgh. It was glorious. The chill made my brain faster. I was heaving oxygen, light headed to the point of soundlessness, as if the energy of my spirit carried my feet to Mach 1. The radiosity of the pores of my skin were like extrasensory eyes feeling the night's cold backscatter.

After four miles up and down Ko Olina Beach, I studied my own musculature under a streetlamp. The setting sun was an eye viewing the pink peaks of my pale arms, like an alpenglow, and my chest, wearing the Belt of Venus.

In this present moment I was following the instructions of some extraordinary exegesis down to the lips of the shore.

This is it. Time to die.

As I was undressing by the coast of the shore, I came up with little goals for myself to lie to the Almighty and avoid the gates of hell.

This is a feat of athleticism, or some sort of bold undertaking. I was going to see if I could swim to Antarctica. That was it. That's what I'm doing.

I was overwhelmed by this irrational desire to swim directly south from Oahu towards Antarctica, and if I died, well, that it is a consequence of my extreme bravery. This can't be suicide because brave people don't kill themselves, because people who want don't want to die, don't end up in hell. Yes I was overwhelmed by this divine impulse, well I shouldn't lie so drastically.

We'll say this. I was driven by a sudden irrational desire to swim to the South Pole. Crazy people don't go to hell. It's not their fault. The insane, in many ways are powerful people in so far as they are given perfect legitimacy to act outside of morays, by virtue of being possessed by that unusual quality.

In fact there is no other expectation than to be scoffed at as a perfect delusive. The insane are, at times, even capable of contending with the articles of faith.

It dawned on me. Yes that's perfect! I'm clinically insane. I was out of control, *AM*, currently out of control of my actions. This is terrible. I can't believe I'm doing this.

I started walking towards the water and the surf came to my toes.

Why was this decision better than going to therapy? Maybe it was unnatural and difficult to be apart of an never ending psychological experiment. Paying this person to get to the essence of me, to synthesize salt from tears in a hot crucible. Maybe I think my therapist wanted me to die.

By going to therapy, I was allowing myself to be made poorer. But I figured the only way out of depression is by action so whenever I started to feel bad I'd get up and start to do things, like going on a run.

It was a sad thought because I really felt myself to be somehow worthy of something. Even some sort of suffering if at all possible. I wanted to let my narcissism get me carried away, or even to have at least one spectator. One person to confirm there was absolutely nothing suspicious about my sudden disappearance to a completely distant continent.

Then I thought about a glorious triumph, wading up onto a prominent iceberg, being lauded by Antarctic scientists as a beautiful specimen of mankind.

While I was making my way into the Pacific Ocean, my final wish had been granted. A kindred spirit down the beach was looking up at the sky, letting the tide wash around her. I watched this woman for a moment, spread out across the beachhead.

"Hey!" I shouted.

There was no response. I reasserted myself. Still nothing.

"I'm about to swim out to sea!" I said. She just looked at me blankly with open eyes. She appeared to be a Hawaiian woman.

"I'm going to swim down to Antarctica!"

I had to assume she only spoke the native language. Still, you see a naked person on the beach and you can't even be bothered to garner a reaction. I worked my ass off all winter for this body.

"I said I'm going to swim away!" Deadpan.

I went into the ocean. It was a remarkable night for such a feat. I would swim until my body floated in an asterism and my dead eyes glimmered dumbly as twin pools reflecting the Southern Cross. I was stepping out into knee height wash. A sharp pain seared my toes. A crab snipped me.

Stepping again and again. Where I was attempting to meet myself with death, where I thought I'd penetrate the amorphous realm to swim out and meet fate, I was met by a walled fortress of crab shells. I couldn't rush to sea. Today wasn't the day. It was too hard and too painful.

Still, it was an unbelievable sight. My feet were shredded up by razor strokes dealt by crustaceans. I watched them carefully while I whimpered back to shore.

The water off their dark red chitin shambled at the brink of liquid glass, and by the time the little shards of water reached the beach edge, the sea had become sand and the sand became crabs.

The coconut crabs stormed the beachhead rooting out of the ocean. How the crabs seized the palm trees and crawled up the multi-headed hydra.

The coconut crabs dehisced several victims, tearing through the fibrous husk, then getting to the flesh. One could admire the slow, barely intentional movements of the coconut crab. As they galloped stupidly up the beach side, I got the sensation that the coconut crab could not be wiped from the sea floors. They are officially understood to be endangered, but for some reason their clumsy movements yielded eons of evolutionary success.

I watched patient crabs rip into the fibrous flesh of the coconut to get to the core of the nut. The animals themselves behaved exactly in the manner of the ocean. Delicately overwhelming the land through their alien patience.

You observe one crab, one wave, and it is about as threatening as the next until the tide is in over your head. They worked away.

Every motion was as slow and clumsy as a wave.

There was no origin to their numbers once they arrived, and the method to the madness was as unintentional as a storm. Not unlike the Boxing Day Tsumami which whisked away countless Indonesian fishing villages, the coconut crabs assailed the unsuspecting palm trees.

The rumors of Amelia Earhart's disappearance are mythologically linked to these creatures. The horror is beyond replication. Hopefully Amelia was unconscious during her steady, bone thorough consumption. Was there a airplane fire? Or did the crabs get right to work after her plane crashed? No matter, a regardless redness overwhelmed the entire fuselage.

For the sake of personal comfort I would like to think that she was not plucked into threads of meat by ravenous shellfish. The idea is too abysmal.

Our bodies, our flesh, are always inevitably carried back to mankind's timeless foe, to the force of nature, with whom we cannot reason. We can barely pretend a mastery over this ultimate pact breaker. Man can make his protestations to nature, but nature denies every compromise. The coconut crab is an interloper of the forces of land and sea. I was considering all of these things as I walked back up to my hotel room.

When I got back, I took a picture of the beach resort, and I sent a mirror selfie to my 620,000 followers.

The caption read, "Guys, I have a confession to make. I almost tried to commit suicide tonight. I know bros aren't supposed to talk about their feelings, but people should see me as an example of why you don't deserve to die. After my racially motivated outbursts last week, I felt so bad that nobody loved me, so I flew out to Oahu to get away from all the hate I whipped up into the world. I'm here to let the world know that it's not suicidal people's fault. It's our society that makes them do evil things."

And with a warm heart I was assured that I could repair my tarnished name. I washed my legs and toes out with peroxide and wrapped them in gauze.

The next morning I woke up happy to fly home that day. Walking down to the parking lot, I got into another rental car. I thought of Amelia Earhart. And then a dreadful feeling plunged into the very heart of me. I left that woman passed out there on the beach.

Down at the shore, she was gone. The waves must have wrested her to sea. It was high tide. My legs, wrapped in bandages, marched back down to where I narrowly feigned my own demise. Did she drown or did the crabs… No. It was like she was never here.

On the way back to Honolulu International the wind was blowing through the sunroof. The sky was beautiful and blue.

It's funny because the truth is I'm a very bad person. When compared to others I can't shake this feeling that I am a scumbag who should roll off the side of a highway embankment and ride into a ditch. That voice is telling me what I did was very wrong and that I deserve to be punished. I should punish myself, or turn myself in for what I did. But it's not gonna happen. I am not going to do that because I am going to survive. Either way it's not my fault. Crabs happen.

I was content because I was becoming the man I was meant to be.

The intrusive thoughts steadily dissipated as I acted in accordance with my nature. Every interesting man is a contradiction. But I don't like contradicting myself because accepting my nature brings me peace.

I don't want to hurt myself because I like myself. And if self-love comes at the expense of others then too bad, so sad. For now, I am boarding an airplane. Better still, I have afforded myself first class serenity of mind.

From that day on I was convinced that I'd been somehow spared in some extraordinarily rare exchange. I had a somber thought on my ride back home, and I have no other way to say it but with great submission to a realization of personal unworthiness. The crabs chose *her* over me.

Before today, breaking old habits or thought patterns was like ripping off a persistent hangnail that I refused to snip. My old dreams, ideals, fantasies stuck to my memory like dead limbs on a deciduous tree. I found myself unhappy in their snipping. So one night I prayed to a higher power, out of personal fear, for a request to let everything that was not necessary fall from me delicately.

And that ripping away character traits by force would cause an odd looking, trauma-spurned growth, as if that same tree had enveloped an electrical wire or a stop sign nailed to it. I prayed to God that if like deer antlers, or baby teeth, or like the lining of a womb, I'd hope to let my hopes and dreams gently abandon me.

It was going to be a problem. They'd find out I left that lady there. Maybe not. I hope they don't. Leaving that lady to the crabs was greatest thing I could've ever done.

Hours passed as the plane flew across the continent.

There was a man's reflection in the plastic airplane window and behind it was the Pittsburgh city skyline. I flew overhead like a lonesome star, imagining the bright airplane migrating across the black sky. For so long I was hypnotized by narcissistic lust. Abducted more like it. Regardless, I had to sacrifice my pride to become a better man. You know what they say, you can't love another person until you truly love yourself.

Before I was just bullshitting.

I said it out loud.

The flight attendant looked at me. So did the passenger behind me. I don't care who heard.

I said it to the reflection.

I love you.

And We Drink The Dead.

Inna Lillahi Wa Inna Ilayhi Raji'un

"I don't want to give a bad impression about myself, that I am a death worshipper, or have anyone lead astray by inquiries into my writings or philosophies. I'll say I am absolutely and unequivocally pro-body. I love life. Look at me, I've built my body well through the discourse of healthful living and fitness. But you cannot criticize me for my work because other people don't accept the realities of bodily mortality." said Mr. Latombe.

The interview evolved into a dance macabre of two voices. Tony felt the jitters of coffee on an empty stomach.

He thought to himself, "What a place to interview such a decrepit old man." He felt the anger of corrupted association, the once upon a time purity of a child's past being desecrated by freshly formed memories. "I played soccer in this church yard, but Latombe wouldn't have it any other way."

"Why do you think that mausoleums are preferable to a plot of dirt?" Tony asked. "If you look right behind us there's a graveyard by the church. As a religious man you must admit your essays against burial are radically unorthodox."

"I find that people are very disconnected from history, especially that which is most recent. Let me tell you a story from my days as a student. When I was young I was extremely romantic, something I find to be so critically lacking today. At the tender age of 22 I was studying journalism just like you. Except near the tail end of college, I received a study abroad scholarship to visit France. It was all expenses paid too. Beginning in Paris, traveling westwards down through

Nantes, and then south to Marseille. Two weeks mostly to myself. I was enthralled at the idea of meeting likeminded poets, to stumble through streets chaste only to my words. They were marvelous times indeed. Here, this is a poem that I published in an old expat journal ages ago."

He handed Tony an original copy out of his briefcase. Handling the amber vellum with careful palms, Mr. Latombe placed heavy emphasis on caution. Cynical Tony exuded in the dogged charade of intrigue, as to not completely abandon his interviewee.

"Please, read it out loud."

Latombe looked eager.

And so Tony read. "Long were the women's garbs, the kaleidoscopic streams of silken liquid, shapelessly pouring out of shops, down a road's cascading bends. Bright peacocks walking riverside to lunch, emblazoned vermillion bolts, bold demonstrations of violet, collared paisleys of Persian gold, emeralds unfair to nature basked amidst a flood of the beautifully dressed people reeking of perfume."

Near the end the dance had picked up gracefully. The lead clung to his pair enunciating each step from his mind. A youthful voice resided deeply inside him, passionately spraying elderly lust upon his Tony's face, who was now even more irritated that the old man's saliva fell on his freshly starched shirt. Tony was in no mood to recite literature and altogether stopped.

Continuing on his own Latombe read, "Carriages wet with pangs of gaudy lacquer, women ornate, men decorum clad, brazenly chieftain eyed, a French avenue, watching and being watched on this very long stage."

"I'm sorry but what does any of this have to do with your mausoleum company, for lack of a better term?"

"Fine. I'll cut to the chase." The old man sighed. "That year I had my first real encounter with death. And it was not adjacent to the spires of Notre Dame, nor in the famed catacombs of morbid curiosity. Not even in the abstract tomes of stoic literature. But it was in the summer of 1926, near the end of my trip, I had to conceal the real purpose of my visit. I needed to find my brother trapped deeply below the poppies of the Somme. Always proud of our homeland by ancestry, my older brother Charles Latombe enlisted as a foreign combatant into the armed ranks of the French Army. He sadly perished on July 1st, 1916.

To speak honestly, he was beyond burial and had been totally dissolved by the bizarre implements of war. There was truly nothing left of him but a letter sent to me the night before he passed. Would you like me to read the letter?"

As an uninvited echo, the voice of the deceased is embalmed eternally in the surviving brother's mind.

Tony listened. "Lonesome, a petal skinned cloud blossomed wearily on the earth's nightside where the gaslike vapors of prayer curdle out of heads through sleeping ears and condense into the atmosphere."

Sleeplessly at night, Mr. Latombe could starkly see in his bedroom's corner, a premonition waking watchfully. He's learned to not twist his head, never to catch a glimpse of the other side.

He spoke his brother's last written words, "Tomorrow the cloud will come and drift over my head and it will rain hard on me."

The interview slowed to a confession and the chamber music had just about died.

"When the sun came up after two days of digging tooth and nail I found only wet dust and that morning I suddenly became strangely ill. It became unbearable to watch that river lining the Somme battlefield, or the scarlet poppies being born out of the marrow-rich soil. I had read that the Ancient Greeks and Hindus had the good sense to at least burn their dead. In my hotel dining room built upon catacombs I drank in the rainfragrant truth of morbidity. As above, so below. It all made sense. I realized in an epiphany, the truth, that the dead crowd the living. They lie thick in the cities. They throng the valleys in which we walk. And obscurely, they mingle with the flowing streams and the running rivers. *And we drink the dead.*"

Latombe's eyes glazed over as Tony's nervous jitters replaced tone deafness.

They went mute, and Tony's eye looked upwards at a silver airplane tearing overhead through the blue slit sky.

"Thankfully for me the mausoleum business will always be in vogue. Even for those bright peacocks walking out to lunch."

Based on the story of Vance Thompson and his essay:
Millions of Dead Poison the Living, Reading, Pennsylvania, 1915.

Ottoman, Autumn

It was 1632. I was taking refuge within the walls of my home city Constantinople.

During the late spring I made plans to take several months off the road to collect and edit writings from my various travels throughout our newly acquired Balkan territories. These writings were then going to be offered to the court scribe for the library of the righteous Sultan Murad IV, and set to be copied for the libraries across his empire.

At the time of Ahmed's attempt at flight from Galata Tower, the tower spanned nine stories. From the very top there offered a vision of the Bosphorus Strait which severed two continents. It was the dividing line between east and west, Asia and Europe. I was looking on from a height by the Sultan's palace and I stared into the Bosphorus. The blue strait's serenity was deceptive. It made me forget the years of fighting that took place here. After all, this was the city where Rome collapsed, who's conquest signified the initiation of Islam's end times.

From times of prosperity, from times of plague, Constantinople's ports delivered and absconded with civilization as we know it. Empires rose and fell within these borders, which is why it was so peculiar to see a man take flight over the Bosphorus itself.

As I was making my way up to the palace, I caught a glance of Galata and I couldn't believe my eyes. A man leapt from the tower and flew like an eagle. A man with wings jumped from our capital's highest precipice, using some device of his own creation and glided seamlessly over our heads. From his balcony, Sultan Murad IV watched one his subjects fly from one corner of Kostantiniyye to another.

The way the Sultan saw it, this unbelievable man's efforts over an unattempted barrier commanded a mockery of God's will. I could hardly see him, but for a flickering second, a man sized fleck glided across a gilded sun. He soared across the strait and swam through the red sky. When he was pulled back down to earth, the Sultan promptly ordered his arrest and the immediate destruction of his flying contraption.

That night in Sultan Murad's court, Ahmed Celebi, sorcerer, scientist, madman, was presented to the our Caliph.

I looked at the unimposing face guarding some strange motive. There is no precedent set in our legal system to judge his crime. Do you imprison a man who is seemingly unhappy with nature? I was looking at a calm angel who'd carelessly brought down the entire Ottoman ire upon his head.

Who could conceive of the boldness of this skinny polymath? His face was scorned by scratches from his hard return to earth and from beatings dealt by the hands of his bewildered captors. He remained taciturn.

What was so horrible about him? During my travels I've seen men perform every act under the sun and still Ahmed Celebi's brief spectacle impregnated our minds with conceptions of the impossible. The Sultan hardly knew whether to behead him on the spot or promote him to vizier.

Caliph Murad, successor of the messenger of God, Sultan Murad, Sovereign Authority of the Ottoman Empire, humble Murad, simple man who has never flown, paced around this young polymath who tested the boundaries beset to us by Allah. Who was this being? What gives him the right to attempt to taste the sky's clime, to covet the night's nameless splendor?

In bewilderment Murad unsheathed a blade and asked the polymath what he thought of the bejeweled sword. Ahmed looked at the sword and silently flashed a smile at the Sultan.

He said, "I have forty pieces of silver and a collection of several books. You will give them to my son Hasan."

In a rage the Sultan ordered Ahmed to be taken out into the courtyard. Palace guards carried Ahmed out into the empty nighttime square where it was cold and deserted except an audience of several soldiers, the Sultan, and myself.

The Sultan, bearing blade, asked the polymath if he wanted to pray. He said no.

"Very well then." Murad raised his sword, and prepared to bear down on his subject's throat; else any man outdo the Sultan in greatness, or even in the conception of greatness.

Ahmed looked passed us. After a steady gust of air blew through wind chimes beneath a bird cage, he saw a hooded hunting eagle perched on a crook in his cage. Ahmed's taciturn face looked at the Sultan who's sword arm was still raised and made one other request.

"That eagle, who will set him free?"

Murad looked at birdcage for a minute. The Sultan ordered me to bring the bird to him and I did. The Sultan handed Ahmed the caged eagle.

"Letting men like you in live is particularly dangerous. You want to fly? You want to assume the mantle of God and the reputation of kings? Well flying man your goal will degenerate angels. Are you so weak in this world that you must flee from it. Are you so eager that you must abandon your Caliph here on earth and take your peace directly to God? You think yourself above us all?" The Sultan paused to think.

He continued, "It only takes only one of you to undermine my empire, to undermine heaven itself." Murad sheathed his sword and dropped the cage at the knees of his unfazed servant. It clattered and scared the bird. "I suppose if you are so selfish to ask polymath, for that eagle's sake, you only ever had the intention of finding out the truth on your own."

Throughout the Sultan's monologue, Ahmed closed his eyes and felt stuck to the ground. He felt a transience in his own abilities, the fearful magnificence of a lightweight heart. As he streamed in the mid-air over the Bosphorus, the cold wind clamored at the sides of his face. The wind became his slave in a personal conspiracy to make Ahmed the most powerful man on earth. His skin felt the breadth of the setting sun, a sun who promised to champion power to the man achieving a happiness beyond the unfenced sky.

The knowledge Ahmed wielded, with just wood and cloth and wire, could turn the whole world upside down. And as soon as he got too ambitious the winds abandoned him and he fell back down on the other side of the strait. If God's light comes down from the stars above, no man was closer to God in the kingdom than Ahmed. And everyone, the Sultan included, marveled at his audacity.

Several days after Ahmed's flight, a fate was decided upon him by the Sultan. Murad awarded the polymath an unceremonious treasure of several dozen gold coins and expelled him to Algeria. It was a difficult decision but Murad did not want to risk slaughtering a man on the brink of sainthood. Though Murad saw a devil in the flying man, nobody in Ahmed's remaining days within the walls of Constantinople laid a cruel hand upon him.

On the day of Ahmed's expulsion the Sultan watched the polymath's boat pass out of the Bosphorus strait.

The Sultan reportedly said. "That is a scary man. He is capable of doing anything he wishes. It is not right to keep such people."

On the way out of the city, Ahmed let his caged eagle fly knowing the bird was not coming back.

Since his banishment I did not hear from the newly revered Eagle of Constantinople. Despite his achievements and his fame preceding him, the polymath's reputation was reduced to little more than a fairy tale. He faded. After dozens of attempts to seek Ahmed out during my own travels, there was almost no trace of him.

Time passed. Histories unfurled. I heard a story from a fellow scribe while on Hajj in 1640. He told me about a Flying Ahmed the Wise who was last seen by some Bedouin merchant trading his food and water for empty scrolls.

The scribe said that Ahmed was completely treasureless, walking southwards into the Algerian deserts, towards the Atlas Mountains.

During my own travels, I've been lead down roads preceding and receding from civilization. I've followed paths ascending and descending from heaven's direction. I've faced devastating horrors and beauties leading always to my supplication at the feet of the Almighty. In the Crimean Khanate I've uttered shock in the slave markets of Yalta, at the sight and smell of iron chains rusted by flesh and blood. As an emissary to the Italians I've seen the Pantheon in Rome, providing me a lifetime of evidence for man's godly origin.

My home Constantinople held its own splendors. These glorious cities were built by men who ransacked God's creation in search of the richest marbles to build pristine palaces to honor The Sublime One. For Constantinople, wars were made on every part of the world to secure loot to fill the capital's palaces. In the latest conquests in Circassia, I've witnessed the receiving end of glory. The people there have been reduced in sons by our wars, yet they are no less loving, no less deserving of praise. We've taken everything from them. There is no material left for them to build temples or marketplaces. Circassian homes are of mud and daub. We've gone so far as to slit and cauterize entire bloodlines, and still in their lands you will not be unjustly harmed.

In Jerusalem, I saw that temple where the Prophet, peace be upon him, made his journey on a horse resembling lightning. Though out of everything I've seen, nothing astonished me so much as the flight of the mysterious Hezarfen Ahmed Celebi.

The Garden of Earthly Delights

When we reached the tip of the Nata River, Bristol was the one who eventually spotted her through our binoculars. A lioness was prowling in infrared on the cool evening terrain.

"Fetch me an arrow." Bristol said.

He knocked it in his bow.

In the darkness I looked at my older brother's face and I saw a man locked into passionless concentration. His breathing slowed, as did mine, but not in the same way. I was afraid of exhaling any used air down wind. In the valley she could sense undiluted fear. The lioness was licking the wind, tasting adrenaline floating abound.

Bristol was snakelike. It was as if his brain could not adapt to a climate of fear. That inborn reflex of fight or flight stirred no emotional reaction within him. I was getting nervous about the possibility of being attacked. He was blind to fear, black eyed about it, seemingly unapparent to the feeling. Growing up, even our parents were unnerved his lack of the concept. Beatings hurt, but the possibility of pain never fazed him.

Pain, in its extremity, dulls the value of intelligence and makes quick work of wit. I studied the dueling scars mapping out stratifications on Bristol's cheeks, mapping out lived experiences from places he's been on past hunts.

My brother lined up his target with a bowscope. Opportunity came when she sprawled out to lay beneath an acacia tree. We took our chance and he hurled a precise shot into the valley's gaping yaw.

"We got the bitch." He whispered.

She ran and ran and ran a little more, and then tumbled down into a painful dry heaving by the time we caught up to the position of her last stand.

"So this is Cecilia." Our guide said. His accent was dense. "This is the infamous beast of Hwange National Park. This is the man-slayer."

She was defiant up until the very end.

She thrashed about, roaring, ripping aimlessly into the thin barrier of air separating herself and her killers. I looked into her eyes. The lioness was ferocious to an emotive point. Instinctively, I felt like we'd done something terribly wrong.

We gathered around a lioness like a dying yellow fire and watched the fading glimmer in her black pearls. I took out my pistol and clicked the safety off.

"No Paul, I don't want anymore holes in this one. This pelt needs to stay intact."

She was inordinately big. At first I was surprised by the her size. She looked too swollen. I saw Cecilia's nipples purse out of her protruding belly.

Coddled in cool moonlight, behind the twilight agony in the lioness's face, I saw her stomach bloated and her eyes reflect deep into Bristol's. I asked the guide if she was pregnant.

"Look Paul, she's a goner either way."

Bristol stood there. The hunting guide didn't know how to justify what happened, so we went quiet. Words are largely worthless in the presence of spilled blood; in the presence of death. A tragic dreaminess grasped the entire scene, as if the misty tails of a nightmare were dissolving into a coarse unbecoming reality.

In mammals there is a certain glimmer in the eye. Something alluding to our nature, our upbringing, perhaps because we've been breastfed. I saw this as an understanding of a suffering we both knew we needed to inflict upon each other in order to stay alive; both coveting a desire to live, to survive against an endless aurora of brutality. I looked at my older brother and what I saw, I was afraid of.

Bristol's inhumane eyes shimmered noiselessly. Where the eyes of mammals seem to absorb light, his sent Cecilia's rage and fear scattering across a glaze of blue oblivion. He stood upright like a man but every ounce of brain matter behind his optic nerves slithered. His eyes, like lake ice at night reflected nothing, could be penetrated by nothing. His eyes could only be investigated up to the blood vessels like cracks in blue intrepid frost, like ships that go no further abreast a continental glacier. I sat looking into a snake's eyes, exploring serene, ambivalent zero.

A snake mother and its offspring share no bond but coincidence. A snake might birth its young just to return minutes later to feast on the fruits of its womb. There is a commonality between the world of reptiles and men; that is to consume. There is no reason not to believe that when left to their own devices, they would not swallow themselves whole. There was no reason for me not to believe that humans beings could not evolve to become venomous.

It took approximately ten minutes for Cecilia to die. I had to vomit.

In the brush, I heard the sawing of a serrated knife and sound of snapping bones. In the corners of my vision I saw Bristol skin her and take her head. Afterwards we walked back to the jeep with our prize. In our wake we left them there, outstretched on the cold plain; ribbons of unborn cats.

I crossed a rubicon of action-association, feeling completely outside of myself. I sat down at our makeshift campsite and started a fire about fifty meters from the dead cat. Death brings with it an actionable sense of world diminishment. Triviality was pervasive with death laid so near. I couldn't sleep so I sat down on the damp ground beneath a forested outcropping. Bristol handed our guide a stack of paper. The guide got in his jeep and was on his way into the night. I don't blame him for not sticking around.

I thought about those little lions and shut my eyes in silence and began twiddling rosewood prayer beads, thinking there is so much work that goes into the making of a human being.

My mom would tell me all kinds of stories about how difficult of a pregnancy Bristol was. I couldn't believe what I was thinking. In my mind I saw Bristol's flesh slowly furnishing bones, encasing them in soft skin. I saw the pulsing web of his ecstatic nervous system blinking, and his brain floating in soft infantile dreams. The way his lips pursed, feline-like, ready to swallow milk.

"One generation passeth away, and another generation cometh: but the earth abideth forever. Isn't that what they say Paul?"

I didn't want to say anything to him.

"You still never quit that shit huh?" Bristol said, as he came floating out of some dry heather. "There aren't too many people like you anymore."

"Sure there are, you just stopped showing up for congregation." I said.

"No there aren't. As far as I saw it was just a lot of guilty masturbators."

He paused to start a cook-fire. The flame slicked back his jowls, revealing an adder's jaw, flickering in slender severance.

"No I'm talking real God fearers man. Ever read that chapter from Joyce with the Jesuit sermon?" He took another moment to take a good look at me.

"I suppose that's one way to put it."

Steadily, I watched him. He held a scowl which drooled of wet blood, or of that dead lion, or of the painted shades of Hieronymus Bosch.

"Yes. I can see you Paul. I'm talking faith. Faith that *the* Jesus Christ is coming back."

A gale from the cliffside echoed into an overlook wider than a man's heart. The wind was carried into the deafeningly empty mopane barrens, which only hours ago reflected *The Garden of Earthly Delights*.

"You hear that?" He asked me. "Then a wind from the Lord sprang up, and it brought quail from the sea and let them fall beside the camp, about a day's journey on either side."

"What are you trying to say?"

"Sounds like us Paul. Sounds like we're pitching up here tonight."

But there was no settling in.

The stars, in all their fanatical fury laid waste to the South African plain. The firmament, in a moonlit assault, left tree-shaped welts on the landscape and battered blows of avian starred bruises across a submissive earth.

"Paul you can hear em' can't you?"

"Yeah the wind, I hear it."

"No. Listen. It's the maggots. They are singing."

We could no longer be called to any innocence. There was a sound to it. We listened to the aching maggots, with their many vocal chords, slaking haggardly at a throat sized wound. Death is an unmatched marksman.

"Are we murderers?" I asked.

"Who's we?"

With that Bristol went to his tent. He was going to go to sleep soundly, not knowing that in several days the whole world will hate him, hate us. I sat there praying for the next day to come.

The next morning we left Hwange National Park and drove back to Harare. From there we caught a flight to back to Johannesburg. By the time we boarded the plane back to Miami, the park rangers had already discovered the body of Cecilia and the unborn cubs.

I saw her on the third page of the *New York Times*. The paper was flipped open on a seat at a terminal at Miami International Airport. It was a blurry shot, to censor anything too horrific. She was in the exact spot where we'd slain her amongst the valley's dry thistle.

The story had already been published before my plane had touched down on the other side of the Atlantic. The photo must've been taken by the park rangers. The body is already headlong into the unyielding process of decadence. Bristol didn't want to look at the newspaper. He said there was no point in looking.

In bold capital letters a headline read:

Pregnant Lion Slain by American Trophy Hunters!

Either way I already knew what she looked like because I went back in the early morning before leaving. Part of me needed to confirm what I'd done. It was a case of doubter's disease. I wanted to deny the responsibility that comes with an extreme fault of action.

It wasn't just a bad dream. I saw her undercut at the belly, at the seat of the soul, where viscera spilled in an outpour of dawn colored streams. Overnight, the dry thistle encroached and random animals fed on lion meat.

Sunburn was achieved in the lioness's eyes. She'd been memorialized in newsprint. I looked because I couldn't stand it anymore.

With the help of every other major news outlet, the whole world figured out who we were within a matter of hours. It caused a minor international scandal between the Zimbabwe Parks and Wildlife Management Authority and the U.S. Fish and Wildlife Service. Both of whom tried to take us to court. Luckily in the end, we weren't charged with anything. I had to take a leave of absence from accounting at my dad's farmland real estate firm. While my brother's dentistry was completely boycotted due to the efforts of animal cruelty protesters. Anti-trophy hunting activists even splattered *lion killer* in red paint on Bristol's home garage door in Fort Myers.

As the protests continued, vegan activists threw pounds of ground beef at his home and workplace. Eventually they got tired of the activism when they finally realized he wasn't even living in Florida anymore.

I was able to handle the occasional death threat and the lambasting but Bristol disappeared entirely. He faded into perfect ambiguity like a column of air or a disease carrying mist, only leaving behind a tracing languor himself. If there was any trace of him, it could be found in the small details of some tortured triptych. He could be juggling skulls in hell for all I know.

A couple months would pass. It would all blow over. People would eventually forget about me and him and even about the dead lion. Well, almost everyone. The moral appetite is always ravenous, but it is also fickle.

I remember one late August afternoon, I was making lunch for my niece who was sitting in the living room watching cartoons. The doorbell rang. Through my front door peephole I saw standing there a young Isabella Marquez. Her tan face stared ignorantly back at me. Ignorant, at least to the minor annoyances she caused on a weekly basis.

I pulled the chained door back just slightly so Isabella could see me.

"What do you want?"

"Hey Paul, I was just wondering if you would be willing to do a follow up interview?" She sounded less accusatory this time. "Things have calmed down since a couple months ago and maybe…"

"Maybe what? If I was willing to be harangued by another shit storm I would've called PETA to come to my address and harass me personally."

"It'll take less than ten minutes. I came all this way." She said.

For some reason I had some sympathy for the girl. I was about to slam the door in her face, but I knew the matter with the cat was basically finished. If there was anything good that would come of all this at least Miss Marquez would get something out of it.

I unchained the door and opened it fully.

"Just sit down at the dinner table. I'll be right there. It's over on the right."

I came back from the kitchen and handed my niece a grilled cheese. I told her to turn down the TV because we had a guest.

My oaken dinner table, up until this interview, avoided all usefulness. It remained an antique of meals with friends and acquaintances long lost. I don't blame any of them for leaving so suddenly.

"I hope you don't mind." She announced her words declaratively after pressing play on a slender recorder. "So Paul, it's been a couple months now since the…" Isabella looked at her notes. "slaying of a pregnant lioness living in Zimbabwe's Hwange National Park. Have your feelings evolved at all on the matter?"

It was as if a lion had become more human than animal, or for that matter, that I'd had become more animal than human.

"Look I get it. I really do. Lions are a vulnerable species. I'm not some moron who doesn't understand consequences. I wasn't then and I'm not now. If anything I've only become more aware of the self-righteousness that separates me and those who think they're pacifistically absolved of violence."

Isabella scowled.

I went through this conversation a hundred times in my head. I offloaded it onto her.

Violence. The word itself made her recoil.

"After growing up big game hunting my entire life you learn that old age is incredibly unnatural. Had we known she was a couple weeks away from giving birth we would've waited. You'll just have to believe that."

"I see." She said. "Don't you think it's a little unfair that…"

"Did you eat lunch today Miss Marquez?"

"What?"

"I said did you eat lunch today? And if so what did you have?" I asked taking a bite into my grilled cheese.

"Yeah I had a roast beef on rye. Why?"

"Everybody eats Miss Marquez, and maybe it's unfair. Have you consulted the 39 million cows that are slaughtered every year. Or imagine our insatiable mouths and every habitat rendered inhospitable for our grain. Your bread. Their bodies for yours."

She was taking notes.

"You know what's unfair? Losing your livelihood because countless mouths are ravenous for morality. And you're the one feeding them. But hey I get that too. We're all entertainers, entertaining the entertaining of entertainers." I exhaled. "Now if you were to crucify a farmer, how pitifully boring?"

"Did your brother tell you that?"

It was an attempt to be condescending, the need to perform a moral push back to save her conscience.

"I don't think Bristol gave a fuck either way. And now neither do I."

My thoughts were pooling out onto the polished tabletop, reflecting back at me. I was looking into my own memories from the night we went hunting.

I could remember how after Bristol went to bed I threw a log onto the campfire. I saw how in seconds counted by cackling pops, furies of minutiae poured out of an otherwise lifeless piece of wood. I watched as freckles of insect life came boiling out from the log's pores. Millipedes and spiders and recluse beetles fumbled out of their tempestuous ambiguity, into the consumptive flame.

Suffused in heat, their exoskeletons withered into illuminations of smoke. I watched ant vapors unfurl upwards. In this minor tragedy, hundreds of insects blistered out of my campfire and were offered up as an omen to who knows what. Semi-subconsciously there was a vision of myself eating lion flesh like some wine-dark hominid, until dawn burst in her blood-red labors. I felt it a sin, deep down, to kill and to not eat. So I had to make it right.

"I'll tell you what Bristol told me and it was a strange thing to say before returning to a reality where you're the most hated man in the world."

"Was it your last interaction with your brother?" She asked.

"We were getting on separate planes in Miami. He didn't wanna tell me exactly where he was going but he said he was sorry because he knew living at home was going to a burden. I knew it was freedom he was after. Last I heard he was going after a snow leopard in India."

I thought back to that day he held me close in the airport. I knew for certain it would be a while before I would see my older brother again.

"I remember he told me that freedom is nothing more than a feeling. It's a transcendent emotion, where with your fingertips you get to push back against the world for a moment. He said most lifetimes are spent fleeing in fear of pain. But for him pain was the secret ingredient and in freedom there is no right or wrong. In the illimitable span of your brief command over life you may come to rule yourself majestically or despotically. If lead meaningfully, you will be eternally attached to those fleeting moments, those little lifetimes, remembered in fervor or in regret. Perhaps this was his explanation for what separates us from animals."

Isabella looked surprised.

"You must understand one thing about my brother, before stepping onto that plane he placed a torn leaf of paper into my care."

I pulled it out of my living room drawer and handed her a folded note. It was a small passage from a Kurdish poet reading:

> *That after loves longingly lived,*
> *And a long list of actions,*
> *You will remain,*
> *Right there,*
> *Impervious to time.*

Parakeets

From a bus window Daniel saw a distant ball of light concentrate turn its eye across Pittsburgh.

"Obsessive compulsions can be very safe you know?" Tommy said.

The moon seemed capable of some benign intelligence. He looked and the moon was intriguing to him; similar to how a child thinks he can reap secrets if he stares at something long enough.This benign creature floated up over the horizon every night to scrape shadows from their orbits around black fires. The moon, pitched in the night sky, looked hungry for yesterday's leftover sunlight. It looked to absorb shadows and send them stumbling lightless into hell washed darkness. These personifications all worked through his worldview as a ceaseless accord of transactions.

"Danny I said I think obsessive compulsions can be very safe."

Two cousins were on their way to work at the Rivers Casino. Tommy leaned towards Daniel's upturned coat collar almost bobbing their heads into one another from a pot hole road bump.

"You can get mad at me all you want, but you can't say my OCD doesn't come in handy."

"Of course you remind me all the time how it might hold you back in life, but like you say…" Thomas chimed in together with his cousin. "*You can never be too careful.*"

The pair sat in silence for a moment. Tommy's nervous leg started to shake and it spilled some coffee out of his plastic lid. The coffee dripped onto Daniel's starched shirt.

"Danny can we still go out tonight?"

"Yeah after we get out of work we can go home and get changed."

Danny still didn't have the guts to tell Tommy that he got fired two days ago, but he was gonna let Tommy figure that out on his own.

"I bet tonight's the night. I'm gonna pull a bad bitch tonight Danny. And you too. Maybe you can find a nice girl to take home."

"Maybe."

"You know Lauren was such a good girl. She loved you so much, but I think it's time for you to move on."

"Tommy no offense but I'm not taking girl advice from a 27 year old virgin."

Daniel looked back outside. He started thinking to himself, "As much as he got on my nerves, Tommy was a good hearted guy. We knew he had some degree of an undiagnosed disability. His parents believed that even if it was true, they didn't wanna limit him with a weakening word.

The funny thing about autistic people is that despite all the rhetoric surrounding the equality talk, our society does everything in its capacity to avoid discussing the sexuality of the disordered. And at the thought's end some clown is already coming to the conclusion that we need to establish Asperger's Sexual Awareness Month. Our job as good people is to eradicate our preconceived notions and unconscious biases against the sex lives of those who were formerly referred to as "mentally retarded". This line of thought is making me neurotic. No. What I mean is the motherfucker just wants some pussy like the rest of us."

Daniel turned to his cousin.

"Man how many times have we been late to work because you had to check the oven so our apartment complex doesn't burn down? Or to take a ride back home to close the fridge several more times to make sure our food doesn't spoil and we don't starve? No candles were lit, the birdcage door is closed so Maya doesn't escape. I don't even know why you care so much, she's not even your bird."

They both knew that the compulsive checking came in handy on one occasion in 2017. Tommy was Christmas shopping with his mother and a cashier accused the two of shoplifting on their way out of a store. Luckily Tommy had a photo of the receipt with the date timestamped to compare with CCTV footage. Tommy's philosophy was that you should keep and document everything, just in case there is a pending lawsuit. Since then Tommy's been a victim of his own confirmed suspicions about people.

The cousins began surpassing each other's voices in volume.

"Danny it's because I care about you. You're not the only one who has problems letting go of things. It took you months to get rid a receipt from the last time you got coffee with Lauren. Besides the only reason you threw the receipt away is because I accidentally dropped it in a puddle."

As of last Tuesday, Tommy was officially jobless and Daniel's young wife had been dead for two years. Both of them were building a wall of memories to keep them from moving forward. The Moltke family crest should state, "Nothing New, Nothing Going Wrong".

Danny looked his cousin in the eyes and said, "I suppose if a stove top gas leak blows us away when I go scramble an egg, everyone will keep in mind how right you were. Also I'm sure Theo will eulogize the proven health benefits of OCD."

Danny's box of date night receipts from his dead wife is not unlike Tommy's list of job application rejection emails in the aspect that they are both good enough evidence to show they took a crack at life. The pain of failure or loss was justifiable enough as long as they had commemorative markers of their own unhappiness. Each one had exactly what the other never wanted. Danny's love lost, and Tommy never loved at all.

"At least you loved somebody." Tommy said.

"At least you're retarded enough to get away with never having to be employed."

Danny's fist clenched up his coffee stained dockers.

Tommy was the first one off the bus.

***

In the dark mirrored casino door there was somebody to taste my breath, wear my head's poorly trimmed brambles, someone to feel the worn instep of my soles, but there was no one inside of the reflection to feel at odds with himself.

The floor manager didn't let Tommy inside. He was late too much and he conveniently avoided all the emails and phone calls made to let him know he wasn't supposed to come here anymore. Theo turned him away at the door.

For some reason every time I get to work I rehearse this Ben Franklin quote in my head, "Most men die at 25, but aren't buried until they're 72." So it's strange to find the same man's image defacing currency enforcing this casino's one rule of law. I think it was Ben Franklin, or the quote itself could be counterfeit.

I looked at the inconsequential patrons inhabiting the casino, perfectly embodying the undead living.

If we are considered to be sculpting ourselves, and you're slamming vodka red bulls until your body vibrates near the mortgage gambling kiosk, you'd likely be considered a hardened compound of wasted wishes. That if considered to be sculpting ourselves, many end up far less than ugly sculptures and a little more than a stab at life pricked by hesitation marks. If anything at all, too many beautiful people become untouched slabs trimmed perfectly for a headstone. In the meantime, their bodies become a medium for the dreams of others. In the meantime, their bodies become a bleeding slab of rock.

I attended the roulette table. Different creatures came up to me taking stakes at numbers or reds and blacks or greens.

One gambler in particular, who'd become a regular of mine, had a terrible grimace on his face every time he came to me. The gambler walked right up to my nest, eyes spangled with lust, expectant to find Lady Luck herself spread eagle. If you caught him in the act you'd see a flabby musculature on the losing side in a struggle against gravity. The face gripping his skull was so atrophied I could've sworn a worm shrugged out of one nostril and up the other. His gambler's face, smiling in the dim light, resembled a man happy to survive a grease fire. Even though he walked away from my table $6400 dollars richer, he cursed winning, and he cursed doubly at failure.

I remember my first couple days working at the casino and how quickly my ideal vision of humanity faded. It's so funny because I always imagined human beings as these progressively evolving things. That craven man disturbed my mistaken assumption that humanity could not evolve backwards. That we may, in a coming era, relinquish our consciousness. Our spines will curl forwards and we humans will become semi-bipedal again. That gambler changed my mind. If you spent evening after evening with him you too would conclude that we were not yet deigned for egotism; or perhaps in our fury out of Eden we'd interrupted the work of angels. I'll never get his name. I never wanted to know it.

At my lunch break I seriously considered what Tommy said to me. I wasn't always such an uptight freak. I didn't hold onto every little comment or detail. But since she died I became prone to the anxiety that God could just take it all back. And after we lowered her into the ground I got to thinking seriously about the here-after, throwing myself into the idea that there is no finer safety than in heaven with God. and no more unrefined terror than to be deceived here on earth. Still I am prone to deception, arrogantly believing that anything here belongs. Most of all I am tricked by the veiled deception that impurity dissolves with time.

What does any of that have to do with roulette? Is that true? It doesn't matter because right now I feel it. For the past two years I had a feeling that I bet my life on love and lost it all.

The end of my shift signaled an abrupt reprieve for 16 hours and with it a reprieve from feigned elegance strained towards drunk bastards who tip poorly. Loose lipped, they would slur insults passed teeth waxed in grime, clenched by gums that would bleed at the mere thought of a toothbrush.

I thanked Theo for my paycheck and nearly succeeded in my beeline for the exit, not before in the corner of my eye I saw something that captured me. In a Swarovski store window display, I saw a pair of crystal parakeets.

Their marvel was so intense that they seemed to transform the foundations of physics. Their presence was of birdsong somehow turned solid, making razor sharp rainbows tweet at every vertex. Their form, somehow self-contained, emanating the essence of the sun, where green-gold matrices form into glass bird feathers.

Staring at the pair, I'd forgotten I'd almost become accustomed to feeding my one remaining pet. Lauren was devastated when Maya's mate flew away and I decided it was time make them one again. Walking up the to the cash exchange, I turned in my whole check and put it all on a single hand of blackjack.

Realistically, an event that decided this month's expenses obliged several minutes of temporary insanity. I could hear a parakeet's kaleidoscopic murmuring in my ear. The birds' shapes are outlined by minuscule supernovae, glistening where each corner fused together, are bright beyond comprehension. They were bright not unlike a description found in *The Tibetan Book of the Dead*.

It says you'll see a light that signals an extinction of illusion. They held a luminosity seen in dreams or supposedly in the Bardo. At this point in my life I had nothing to lose and having nothing to lose steals you from a fear of losing anything at all. At this point it wasn't even gambling.

In front of me was the four of clubs.

The dealer had a queen of hearts.

Hit. Five of spades. Hit. King of hearts. 19.

The dealer turns his card. Eight of diamonds.

My 19 to his 18.

This was the only time I've ever gambled. I tossed him some chips and came away with $5,800. I took my winnings, walked up to the Swarovski retailer and paid for the crystal birds outright. It was Lauren's birthday tomorrow. They were the perfect gift for her.

At 11 PM I took the bus home and got changed out of my work uniform. I got into some decent clothes and called Tommy saying that I would meet him outside the Liberty Street Bar in a couple minutes. Tommy beat me to it as I walked up the road.

I could tell he was nervous. He was playing with the wheel on a disposable Kodak camera. The clicking and the flash and the clicking and the flash. A nervous habit.

"Daniel what took you so long?"

"Sorry man I was just getting changed and the bus was late."

"I don't think I wanna go inside The last time we came here I almost got into a fight and well I just don't think it's a good idea." He was about to walk away and I stopped him.

I started laughing. "Yeah Tommy because that guy thought you were taking pictures under his date's skirt. Put that thing away man it's sketchy"

"I wasn't I was just nervous." He put the camera away.

"I bet there's at least one cute girl in there."

That made Tommy laugh too. We went inside the bar.

After a couple drinks, he loosened up. I always enjoyed building up Tommy's confidence every time we went out together. For the past couple months he was finding no success because he'd get too bashful and spill the beans that he never kissed a woman before.

Drunk girls would coo "Awwws" at Tommy if they didn't creep away from him.

The Smiths' "How Soon is Now?" flooded the speakers and caused a clamoring at the dance floor. Success. He snuck up behind a pretty drunk girl and laid into her ears with his coy chantings. There was no one mediocre in sight. Tommy was human and needed to be loved.

They were both hammered and her arms curved up above his shoulders and around my cousin's black hair. Tommy's hands slendered down her hips, smocked in vodka and velvet. You couldn't imagine the glamour on his face. It was glorious. As they danced, Tommy looked at me with a love intoxicated smile on his face as the pair fumbled out of the bar. Thank you Johnny Marr. Thank you Aphrodite for taking mercy on a sexless order obsessed innocent.

As I watched the indecent pair get into a cab headed towards Shadyside, Tommy's camera fell into a puddle of rain. He didn't think twice about it. I didn't need to stick around anymore. It was 2:30 AM and I walked home. I knew tomorrow held something in store for me.

Down the street I trudged through my neighborhood. One step after another, frame after frame, tall buildings paneled into homes. Windows lit up apartment buildings, glistening in their own light like wisteria, trickling deep down into different views of everyday life. I was looking inside windows catching glimpses at families fallen asleep on the couch, or at lonesome TV viewers staring at a pleasure hearth, or at others somewhere in between. While I knew Tommy was having the time of his life, I couldn't shake the opposite inclination. My entire walk home seemed shaded in the lived actions of a distant life. It was déjà vu or a reoccurring dream.

In dreams we have the highest difficulty drawing upon memories from either waking or sleeping reality. In dreams everything is being done for the first time, then being immediately forgotten. Tommy was losing his virginity, and I was coping with absolute loneliness for the first 745th night.

My alarm clock rang the next morning. It would've have Lauren's 26th birthday.

I got out of bed and fed Maya and I got the crystal birds that were wrapped up so carefully, with it enveloped a little letter prepared some nights ago.

In my dream I saw her. At the entrance of consciousness, I wondered with what savagery the gatekeeper slays memories trying to cross from the waking and sleeping worlds. At his behest I am dependent upon a scythe to guard vagrant memories from slipping by both thresholds so that dreams, conscious and unconscious, do not become one.

I've fallen in love in a dream, I wept because I did not want to wake up. There was some woman I've locked eyes with before and was not sure at which exit I left her. So at either gateway, I march through the world waking and sleeping looking for my love, lurching for crumbs of memories, my eyes gangling dreamlike.

I felt like I was waiting to arrive at the next world. My heart's investments are locked up in transit between this stopping point and the next. She has the car keys at the next stop in a far off land where you don't speak the language and you've never set foot but she's waiting. The only thing you know is that a trolley is coming and you'll be riding alone for now.

My aluminum blinds creaked and I looked out the window. A bough drooping spice clung to the air.

Late autumn, austere as a flame, lit leaves upon trees casting a tessellate smolder over morning clouds. The morning snow illuminated my walk to the cemetery. Snow falling is snow ablaze.

When I got to the cemetery I took out the beautiful parakeets and laid them at the base of Lauren's grave. Above her headstone there is a maple tree. Underneath my feet, her body fed a maple prepared for late fall. At the tip of its leafy crests, wind peeled back red foliage leaving behind a dry system of veins, a body drained of blood. Up on the cemetery hill a sparrow's congress stirs the air, still with fragrant fog. I read the name etched into the grave marker and thought it might as well be mine.

This gift was so precious because I wanted to think God made us in pairs. I took Lauren's beautiful birds to offer back to her. Just as I removed them from the wrapping tissue, the glass birds slipped out of my hand and smashed on the headstone.

The muscles in my neck drooped babylike, barely held together by a skin rag, with a mind as infantile as the skull constraining it. I started gripping the dry grass coddling the grave and I started to cry.

I started thinking about reincarnation because I was desperate to find anyway back to her. I'm supposed to see that reincarnation is an experiment of thinking. It's designed to keep us from fucking up again and again. We're supposed to realize we want out, but the reason I think about reincarnation is because I have the strong suspicion that I've been dazzled by the same spirit for ages. That I've been seeking out the same hands for centuries. I can't stand the idea, even in a past life, before or after this cycle, that I've been loved by anyone else. And if I had the chance to be with her again, I could excuse the cycle of living and dying and living and dying. So I laid there, belly down on the grass, hoping I would die. Instead I fell asleep.

Out of this sleep there was a palm rubbing on my back.

"Come on Danny. Let's go home."

The voice in my mouth was like an anxious child's.

"She would want you to live. She would want you to be happy." Tommy said.

I flipped over and looked at the sky and closed my eyes and heard a choir of birds singing.

Their inalienable song, carried by blowing wind, cascaded down my lungs like cool liquid. When my breathing finally settled, my soul felt a washing calm of one that relinquishes the urge to return from whence it came.

The Janus Well

"Sean let me give you some advice, this might go against what your mom would tell you, and I'm only telling you this because I had to learn the hard way."

He stopped abruptly to roll down the window of his station wagon and check the mailbox as we pulled up to the cabin.

"I bet a lot of people were telling you how much potential you have. That's because you're a smart kid and you do have potential. But this should be something to keep in mind. Don't let what you were, or who you could have been, mess up who you are right now."

"Mom just wants me and Gilbert to get into good schools." I said.

"Gilbert isn't even in middle school yet. And you've barely finished up high school yourself. What I never understood about that woman, or anybody else for that matter, is their inability to let qualities stand as they are. I've known plenty of good people in my life, lots of them had what your mom would call "potential" and most of them squandered it. With that being said some others became very successful people."

"What about you Uncle Tony?" I could tell that question sent him down a familiar avenue of thought. "Would you say you're successful or not?"

The wheels rolling the red car disrupted puddles in the gravel driveway.

"Well, I get to do what I love everyday and get paid. Isn't there something to be said for that?"

That explanation sounded agreeable enough at the time. I've been thinking for awhile now about what I wanted to do for money. I told my parents that I was interested in law school. Nowhere in particular. It just became a foreseeable excuse for me to read books, and feign progress at their expense. Political Science is a path towards grad school. So I applied and I got accepted into the University of Vermont, as well as UMass. In retrospect, many things I've found myself deciding to do at the time were neither exactly preferable or distasteful.

After we got out of the car we walked up a slender tile path gardened on either side by flowers anticipating sunlight. They were marvelously well kept. Celosia flowers stood about face against the wooden cabin with their aureate heads gleaming aflame.

Cadres of celosia burned at various temperatures.

I remember elegant castle scarlets, yellow cockscombs, and silver blossoms piked along the dirt path up towards his porch. I slowed down and saw a redness in the crested faces of those flowers. Closing in on the castle scarlets, I spied a red that ripped tenaciously through the delicate world of sight. The celosia broke through the gauntlet of the common senses. They were exuberant to a point of singing.

Gilbert was walking sleepily behind me and tugged on the backs of my jean legs as we walked into the house together. I turned, and as my baby brother closed the porch door, I saw wind blowing up withered petals and scattering them like black snow. The dry petals suffused with sunlight and flew away.

Uncle Tony told me to put our stuff in the guest bedroom where two cots were been set up for us.

I picked up Gilbert's things and I set them on his bed.

While Gilbert is only my half-brother, we are spiritually the same. And I took every precaution to take care of him, even better than myself.

Tony came to the door frame.

"Sean can I get you anything?"

"Yeah I'm pretty hungry. What time are we gonna order dinner?"

"I can make something." He said.

I don't recall in particular what we ate, but we ate it quietly while my little brother slept in the other room. And as we finished up, I went to the window sill to shut out the cold and he came up next to me.

"You're very lucky to have your brother with you know?"

"Yeah I know." I looked at the hairless crown of skin in the back of Tony's skull, where he used to tell us he had eyes behind his head.

"I just wanted to let you know I'm happy to see you guys so happy together."

"He's like my other half." I said.

"I have some fun things planned out for tomorrow after breakfast. We can go on a hike and go fishing."

"Okay that sounds good."

We stayed out on the porch, watching the sun creep down around the borders of earth at the limits of heaven's extremity.

"Tony I'm pretty tired I think I'm gonna go to bed."

"Okay bud. Do you need anything?

"No, I'm okay."

"Alright I'll wake you up tomorrow. Sleep tight."

I tried to feign sleep. The bedroom door was cracked slightly so I could see slivers of shadows skirt around footsteps. This was his painting time.

It took me quite a bit of time afterwards to understand the roots of my uncle's inspiration. We all saw his paintings, how grotesque they were, how he didn't want to speak of them.

I crept ever so gently up to his studio and peered inside. It was empty. Empty of humanity at least. Laden within, paintings of every two headed creature imaginable burdened the walls and the tables. Twin headed birds and dual faced dogs littered the studio floor. In medically accurate depictions, some skulls were completely separate from one another, perhaps one head merely clung to the main body, the other remained annihilate of consciousness. Or an entire being would split itself in half echoing the dual wills of siamese twins.

On Tony's easel I saw a Janus faced boy, poignant in his resemblance to its author. His infant face had been stretched apart in slow motion during elastic development, then frozen at birth. The Janus Boy held eyes developed at each end of his face, in sacrosanct liminality, eyes on either side like a horse's, then connected by one large oval eye supplanting both heads. Imagine two fetuses in engaged in dual for sight in which both developing heads were tugging at an over stretched sight organ. Their desire for sight tore the organ beyond utility. All of these images are of fertility gone awry.

"Well you might as well walk in." He said.

So I did.

"I must confess I'm embarrassed for anyone to see what I do."

I looked around, surrounded at all sides by creatures mutilated in circumstance. These silent mutants were crafted painstakingly by Tony brushing away at canvases all throughout the night.

"Get a good look and when you're ready come with me." He said.

"Uncle Tony is that your little brother?"

"Yeah that's him."

I stood looking on at the painted threshold of this poor bastard creature. And looking on and on, I thought I caught a glimpse into the chaos that unfolds behind the mind of this mysterious relative.

I didn't want to think the subject matter of Tony's Janus creatures; half-raptured, half-twinned, totally disturbed, came from reality or from his own brain. Standing around in the studio, I was studying squirrels slivered in two, or at body parts arranged to resemble a centipidal raccoon, or an impression of Frankenstein's rabbit.

At times it is unfathomable to observe the abject difficulties nature places at our feet. Here, all around me, paintings and confessions of failed potential glared at me mutedly.

"If you want a more honest answer Sean. No I am not successful by the classical definition. No I don't make a lot of money. I am here all by myself, painting macabre creatures to sell to clients who want to financially endorse their macabre interests. And it would be nice if I could pretend I could do things the normal way. But here we are. So I might as well spill it. This place is where I grew up. These paintings, this land, this cabin, where I was born, is all I know."

I was hesitant.

"I'm sorry I didn't mean to intrude." I said.

"It's okay, this place is apart of who I am. This place has lead to some plentiful inspiration over the years. Come with me. Let me show you something."

So I followed him as he walked quietly towards the small living room, and out the front door.

"Shhh He's sleeping." He said, not wanting to wake up Gilbert.

The screen door, leading outside to a path past the celosia flowers, creaked slightly.

I traced Tony's steps outside, and followed the timid beam of his flashlight illuminating the back path. Through trusses of branches and past stark bushes we walked around the cabin to a well boarded up by old planks.

Tony whistled.

"Just wait. He'll come."

I was dead terrified at this point. My fear of what was coming couldn't be matched by an abject shock of what rustled up from around a decrepit wood. It was a dog. A dog with two heads.

"Here boys. Come here." Tony whispered. "Come here."

He pulled out two dog treats and fed one to each mouth. A golden retriever, with two independently eager heads began lapping at his hands, licking crumbs off his fingers.

"Do you want to pet them?"

I had absolutely no idea how to greet this derangement. It behaved like any dog I've come across before, almost in the exact manner of any golden retriever thats's been showered with a suburban lease on love. It was still young and puppylike.

"Here… Here's some treats."

Tony put the biscuits in my hand and the dogs heeled up to me. Its tail was wagging.

"Sit Janus."

A golden retriever with two heads sat on its hind legs. I got a close look at it and there were definite signs of horrible deformities, outside of the obvious. One head's tongue drooped low and bowed and whimpered in regards to the other more developed skull, who maintained control over the body. The dogs barked and I jumped and I dropped the treat. After one head ate, I dropped another for the other mouth. It came up to me. I petted the dogs.

"Good boys." Tony said.

After five more minutes of this lesson in abominations, the blood drained completely from my face and I turned around and walked up the path fully disgusted by everything natural. Natural. What is natural? What is the meaning of this word?

I had to laugh. I think I did. I would've never predicted the stupid affability of Cerberus, who light-heartedly guarded the gates of Hades.

Tony dismissed his pet. From up the path I turned to look at him. He was leaning up against a well, on the stone masonry detailing the cistern. The flashlight ray was aimed at my chest.

"They're not the only ones Sean." He said sternly. "Look around on your way up and see a bird. Or a rat."

"Tony I feel sick. I wanna go home."

"You are home. This is where our family comes from."

"Tony you're sick."

I looked into his eyes. I was terrorized by the deteriorating lack of understanding in his face. This blackness in his eyes was an innocence from hell. His lack of concept of right and wrong was the innocence of an ignorant child. The innocence of a wolf is all an innocence from the knowledge of good and evil.

"Wanna guess why I don't have any kids Sean?"

"I don't wanna be here anymore."

Disorientation sank into demanding retreat.

"It's because occasionally creation is not so gentle. It is not so kind. Creation punishes. Creation decays. I've seen many creatures drink from this well. I've seen them in a rush to expel the fruit of their womb. To flush out the products of their gene pool. Do I think there's something superstitious about this water? No. And there doesn't need to be. Do I need a scientific explanation to detail the magnanimous chaos on display? Must I categorize and explain the workings in the war of life against atoms and stars? Look around you. Hear the animals, the potency of life, their potential. Sean I'm going to promise you I'm going to destroy this well. But I needed to confess to someone, to anyone, that something so incredulous could also be so intrusive."

"I feel very ill. I'm gonna go inside. Tomorrow we are going to call my mom so I can go home."

You'd read this and wonder what he put in my food and frankly I wish I was drugged, but going to sleep that night I remember being perfectly lucid. I went to the guest room without any further conversation of what I'd just witnessed and kept a close eye on Gilbert sleeping soundly across the slender room.

As I walked in overwhelmed I woke up Gilbert.

"Is that you Sean?"

"Yeah I had to go get a drink of water."

"You were gone for a really long time."

"It was a very long drink of water."

He was in the haze of sleep.

"Just go back to bed."

Gilbert's long brown sprouts curled over in his pillow and he started snoring again.

I watched him carefully, afraid of what could happen to him.

At my bedside I saw the piercing nettles of starlight pulse through the cabin window. I was so tired. My eyes closed as the moon's spearlike wan slit the tethers of gravity, letting my muscles drift weightlessly with me into a dream.

The next morning, as if out of a feverish madness, I woke up facing an absent bed. I began to panic. Thank God Gilbert came into the room and told me that Tony was going to drive us home after we stop for breakfast.

I didn't have any words to share with Uncle Tony. It felt like some mutual secret. A morsel of information that we both knew was too surreal too expose.

Speaking of it under any circumstance would be beyond belief for human ears. Like the paintings of two headed dogs from the visions of an increasingly mad artist, the haunted details of my life would remain ghostly.

We went for breakfast and I got eggs.

One of those over easy twin yolks came out on my plate next to some hash browns, and its sticky residue threw me back into dizziness.

"That's good luck!" Gilbert said. And I looked at him, past him, like something I could never describe had gone horribly wrong.

"Are you okay buddy, you look a little green around the gills?" Tony asked.

"Yeah."

I forked the twin yokes and burst them free into mucus and yellow.

It was a quiet drive back down from Locustdale, Pennsylvania in the coal region where Tony lived all by himself.

We were near Centralia, PA. It is a tiny strip of land in the Ridge and Valley Appalachians. Centralia was built over a strip mine shaft system which became a trash dump, and in 1962 a trash fire ignited the coal veins beneath town.

The Centralia coal mine fire is an invasive colony of fallen angels establishing themselves beneath penitent normalcy. Now the town of Centralia is totally abandoned, but the fire will burn for the next 250 years.

Back in Allentown, Tony dropped us off while our mother was at work. We said goodbye and as we walked up to our apartment stairs, he called out to us.

"Hey Gilbert, I almost forgot to mention, tell your brother he really missed out this morning!"

Gilbert giggled.

"On what?" I said.

"He'll tell you about how cold the well water tasted."

It was the snake like grin again. The view into bottomless eyes. Eyes with a distinct malice. It was a wry smile given by an insane innocent.

"About what?!"

He pulled away.

I turned to Gilbert.

"What did he do to you?"

"Sean what are you talking about?"

"What about the well?"

"Nothing he just showed me it!"

"He showed you it and what?!" I was screaming at this point, shaking my seven year old brother in exasperate fear.

"He let me get a sip of the water."

The night my mother came home I confessed to her what I saw, what happened with Tony and the well. And the next day I ended up with the school counselor. And the day after that the cabin burned down. There was no diagnosable evidence of his derangement, besides any of his surviving paintings.

Nothing grew from Tony's legacy, and I was stunned by the realization that he was a goner. It was as if the soil over his grave had been salted. To my own surprise he'd kept his promise and sledged the well in.

I spent some time in and out of various therapists and on strange internet forums and inside open ears describing what I saw. It all was to no avail.

Mom, Officer Drake, Dr. Rubinstein, Sasquatch_Hunter65, or any biology professor I'd come across all told me to various degrees that I was a bullshitter, either by omission, accusation, or conspiracy, and that I ought to drop it.

I'll tolerate that from most but as the years passed, the idea that I was the victim of a twisted plot connived by an impulsive freak show was slowly uncoiling me. My secret suspicion is that Tony was intentionally feeding his experiments this poisoned water that was somehow contaminated by the local underground coal fire disaster. I think it was causing horrific birth defects. I thought that after so many of Tony's experiments maybe some lived? That rational explanation gave me enough breathing room to eventually stop scratching my skin raw. Then again, maybe I was being fucked with from the grave. There had to be a sort of scientific solution, a positive explanation that was beyond me. Nothing supernatural.

After about a decade or so I'd manage to get my nervous ticks under control. I was 29 approaching 30, childless, no plans of marriage, and subconsciously sequestered from regularity. Tony's death eclipsed my life.

In my own time I'd gone well out of my way to retrace his habits, to understand his frame of mind, but it's damn near impossible. I go back every once and a while to traipse around the ruins of the cabin, keeping a close eye on the wild life, looking for any signs of his presence there. I couldn't find anything meaningful.

I'd return to the cabin site each July. Gradually, the celosia's many faces grew out of control eventually forming a large meadow. As the years drew by, the seedlings of one event grew into a vast field of heads populating an abyssal pink. One day in the glimmering summertime sun I walked out and stood amongst this field of unfurling reds, shouting at their peak of their powers. I wondered what had driven Tony to such unnatural obsessions?

I laid down in the middle of the field and looked around the meadow from the ground up, as if I was lodged within a concave dome where each flower made up a reflection of ten hundred faces.

In the red field I reared my eyes upwards at the unlimited sky where not even a gesture of a cloud stammered at the endless recitation of blue.

I'll never forget the way that dog ran up to me, totally unaware of its hideousness.

I had this thought that struck me, regardless of the profundity, about how a flower field or the sky staring back at you is incoherent of your suffering, is incoherent of innocence, and is seemingly untouched by the conception of good and evil.

The savagery of natural innocence surpasses evil, it is beyond goodness, and marks the impassible barrier separating me from my concept of Tony. He blanked out on Judeo-Christianity. He's a phantom chimp who'd become unwittingly fascinated by the idea he could deform creatures at will. Not godlike, not scientific, but casually unaware of the suffering he inflicted, though completely enrapt by his fascination with it.

Imagine an ancient ancestor, who causes celosia-like forest fires to spread across the landscape, merely on account of interest, merely because of the satisfaction it gave him to burn the forest to the ground. To some extent, they were all on the equal up until a point of consciousness. They were the same; the ape, the sky, the flowers alight, with no concept of mind, with no image elusive, with no escapist illusions to imagine. I had another thought, enough was enough for one day.

Years later I was doing landscaping work up in the Pocono Mountains. It I was while driving home from a small town called Coalvale that I got a call from my mom. Gilbert's wife Cassandra was having her baby at Lehigh Valley Hospital in Allentown. I made the drive down just in time.

I was nervous and overjoyed, walking into the ER I saw Gilbert who faced me in the waiting room, looking like a despondent prop who'd found no use for his humanity.

A nurse pulled me to the side.

"You must be Tony."

"No no, my name isn't…" I stopped for a second. "I'm the baby's uncle."

"Mr. Girard, I'm very sorry to tell you but your nephew was born with a very rare disorder. It will cause quite the disruption to his ease of life." She continued in a wispy tone until I all but phased her out. "It's called craniofacial duplication and"

I couldn't hear anything.

And out of my mind's eye, a solitary blackness arose. It was a vision. A man painting a baby brusquely at a canvas, and he turned to me, just as he did so many years ago.

A smile slithered up his lips. His eyes slit nihil. He nodded his head and beckoned me with a brush.

Come paint Sean.

The Brazen Bull

"Honestly it was never totally clear how far we'd go. Certainly as far as we needed to. To any extent necessary." I said.

Philip took a drag from a menthol cigarette and pitched it to the curb.

I continued. "While we were living together we were junkies. We took that mentality with us wherever we went. It makes perfect sense that we ended up in the kitchen."

"The kitchen saves more than the church in my experience." Phil said, before taking a sip from a highball glass.

The effects of vodka had pitted us against our resolve to never surrender.

And *Never Surrender* was the mantra etched onto our knives, given to us by our mentor Delamuerte. After we'd enlisted in the services of The Brazen Bull, you'd think we were ex-members of a paramilitary organization, or an El Salvadorian death squad, rather than chefs working in restaurants.

The intensity of our work felt about the same and the magnitude of the mind behind the movement was, by prerequisite, megalomaniacal. Unlike modern militaries, our goal was to ensure that the results of our labors were everlasting. Governments come and go. No big deal. We were working in a different dimension, pushing the boundaries of the culinary experience. Malcolm knew this.

Yes, states are crafted, are digested, and pass through the bowels of history, but it is only several times a century that a restaurant will be awarded three Michelin stars.

Malcolm was my cousin and The Brazen Bull was his brainchild.

I took another swig of vodka, swishing it around my gums, letting the alcoholic sharpness dry out my tastebuds.

I looked at Philip and he looked back at me. I could see the disarray forming around the corners of his mouth. It was disarray caused by drink, but more by confusion. The sides of Phil's face were worn down into a heavy frown.

Cars were streaming by on a nearby highway, grating over concrete cracks like carrots on a rasp. I was already thinking about cooking. We were stateless men. Philip and I had no liege, no master for whom to wield our blades. The entire staff was ordered not come in next week. It was a not so subtle announcement for the unofficial closing of our restaurant.

This reminds me of the Japanese story about the forty-seven ronin, who's sole characteristic of existence surrounded a vendetta after the death of their master. But there was nobody to get revenge on, so there was no point.

I was back to square one. Homeless again. I finished my drink, paid my tab, and I looked at Philip, who was already in the process of falling back down to earth from his place amongst the culinary stars. I patted him on the shoulder and I told him I'd give him a call soon.

It was dark out. Pittsburgh's shifting night lights scrambled my sense of time. I was glad it was night and the day was done. Getting a drink was a reprieve from life as the art of memory making, from the scrutiny of suffocating in the sunshine.

I hailed a cab and it took me back to my disheveled apartment which, strangely enough, was just like the one from the starting point of our story.

At the end of this sentence, the memory of Malcolm Krieger took me right back to where we began.

***

In 1998, long before the opening of The Brazen Bull, long before the Michelin stars, long before I had an unlimited access to a worldful of ingredients, I had only one image in my head, and it was a memory that was scantily recreated.

Distantly, I can imagine Malcolm smashing a rodent's body with a tire iron, and then skewering it, and setting it to char over a barrel fire.

I hope I was too strung out for that hallucination to be true, but I could've sworn we came close to hunting rats to eat in our tenement room. I don't think Malcolm would've even remembered if I asked.

One way or another it didn't matter because all I wanted to do was ribbonize my brain. My logic was shredded into tatters. I was like a rodent in a science experiment pressing the option for more electroshocks and dope. Food became scarce. The attitude is wicked. You'd think you'd starve to death if you had the option between heroin and eating.

In an apartment I rented with Malcolm and our friend Marvin, I learned a brutal lesson in economics. For anyone on living on 16th Street in Newark at the time, money was first and foremost a formality. Our landlord was constantly stomping upstairs and he always got his payments in advance because we'd steal to pay him. Likewise my relationship with food was one of theft, was one of heroin.

We'd organize raids on corner stores for things to sell, and occasionally for something to eat. In retrospect, I learned that human beings often reach a late stage poverty, who like fucked up science experiments, begin eating one another.

I learned about supply and demand. I learned all about consumption in terms of sickness and in terms of ourselves as both the product and the consumer. We become the raw material. Poverty studied scabs on my body, etching the masterworks of *Das Kapital* and *The Wealth of Nations* into my subconscious.

In desperation, Marvin resorted to selling his body to sordid types who sat slightly higher on Maslow's Hierarchy of Needs. Outlines with money hobbled into our squat, woke up Marvin, threw a fiver on the frameless mattress and took him to rent in the bathroom. Marvin would gamble himself in dice games and a lot of the times he lost.

Then one day after several weeks of abuse, tantamount to slavery, he disappeared, and with him disappeared any likelihood of maintaining the impression we could pay rent.

Another day, not long after Marvin vanished, Malcolm came home with heat and shells. It was a revolver, surplus from God knows what war. Fuck it. Let's go hunting.

Me and Malcolm lurked in abandoned abodes. On the outskirts of 16th Street, neighborhoods suffered a poverty like desertification. Imagine getting held up at gun point by twin bodhisattvas admonished by a hunger past fasting. We wove ourselves into a history before thought. Our bodies ate into our muscles, into the marrow of our bones. We traversed back to the time of the first humans. Junk smacked us pre-historic, back to when we first developed tools to smash open bones to suck marrow dry.

I liked serving bone marrow when we first opened up The Brazen Bull in Pittsburgh because it reminded me how the survival instinct inspired gene pool altering decisions. But in January of 99' we got kicked out of the tenement.

Me and my cousin were officially homeless. Worst of all we didn't even have money for drugs.

We were very close to death at the time. I didn't know it yet but a restaurant would save my life. I don't mean this in the laborious sense either. Before I even got a job, me and Malcolm would gather trash bags from barber shops and dry cleaner dumpsters and stuff our clothes with human hair or drier lint to insulate ourselves.

While digging out of the dumpster behind a steakhouse called Le Cheval we found out about an air vent that let out steam from the cooking line. We hunkered down there, just behind the alley, letting the smell of angus beef engulf us. It kept us alive throughout the dead of winter.

Lint tatters and hair shorn from sideburns and hemmed shirts began to fully emulsify with umami. It kept me shivering, a flavor profile like chemicals, salty tar, and brown butter. All the while I was riding out an addiction I couldn't supply. Luckily for us the part time dishwashers got deported and Le Cheval had to resort to hiring dope sick vagabonds. Somehow we got hired. We would've starved if the manager had never gotten us jobs scrubbing pans.

From dishwashing I worked my way up through salads and desserts, from meal prep to pastas, and in a period of five months I was dressing filet mignon for Newark's finest.

Suddenly money began to appear in my wallet because didn't have to support an abusive relationship with a junk habit.

By the following November, I moved into my own place. I didn't have to bum it with friends, or distant relatives, or people who owed me a favor.

The first thing I did before I went to sleep in my own bed was bolt the doors shut. The second thing I did was form a budget. I was making a clean $900 bucks a month from working as a line cook. After rent and utilities I was allowed to imagine what interests felt my wallet's gravitational pull. I remember that word wallet was another funny object to remember, considering those times. I was more likely to gnaw at the leather than carry around a "please stab me" bulge protruding from my back pocket.

After my bills, I had over a 200 dollars to spend on myself. Ingredients galore. Best of all I was finally eating enough to be classified as slightly underweight.

My first knife was given to me in Newark by a friend, chef Oscar Delamuerte. He was stocky and had hammer like hands. He taught me how to use the sabrelike Damascus steel. The knife's crisp design shivered in accordance to the rhythm of my pride. I felt very well armed. It was tidy, surgical, and cut as smooth as rushing water.

***

He called me when I woke up the next morning at around 11 AM.

I remember it was late September near the end the day when I last saw him. He came into The Brazen Bull to witness the work of his students, to see his influence for himself. Oscar is a tall, broad bodied, fat Mexican man, who couldn't have had a more profound impact on Malcolm and me if he tried.

Aside from inadvertently saving our lives, he repurposed us for ardent use in cookery. The name of Le Cheval came from a joke between Oscar and his Aunt Valeria.

Before Oscar came to America, his Aunt and him ran a taqueria. One night when they had ran out of pork for carnitas so they sold horse meat to unwitting Cancun spring breakers. The customers loved it.

Oscar was in town for the funeral yesterday and we met up for lunch at Ritter's Diner around noon. For the first time in my life, food was not the one urgency intertwining us.

It was unusual to see this cavalry general of a chef so pale, but he smiled to see me, and embraced me whole heartedly. I looked carefully at the man who taught me everything I knew and I saw how vaporous he'd become, like a father who lost a son.

We sat at a table. A waitress took our order.

"How are you my boy?"

"Not too good."

"That was a nice service they had for him."

"Yeah, it was."

The day he died felt like the day of the apocalypse. And today for some crude reason the world is still turning. And the world will keep turning, and I will remain here, mind paused, with no time to start again.

"Ryan, there might not be much to say right now but…" He was reaching into a leather bag. "I came here with something that I think will be very valuable to you."

Oscar pulled out a little red notebook. It was bound with metal ringlets, caught up at the left side with paper fringes.

"I think I know what you're feeling. You might think you don't know what to do. But he left this behind. I'm not sure what to call it. A manuscript? Cook book? We found it cleaning out the office."

Oscar handed it to me. Wiping his eyes, and then he began to smile slightly.

"Malcolm was a madman."

I grinned at Oscar but I desperately wanted to see what was in inside and I started paging through it.

"I think you're better off looking on your own first."

"You're probably right." I said.

"Hey, do you remember that service with the Russian apple?"

"Yeah, that was the one that put us on the map."

We were both smiling.

"I remember the look on the bastard's face when we brought out desert." I said. "We served our most prominent guest to date, a Russian VP from the Kalashnikov Concern, an antonovka apple."

After doing careful research we discovered he had a debilitating allergy to a variety of apple grown specifically in Kursk. While in the KGB he famously survived numerous poisonings, so naturally we served the old bastard his own personal cyanide on a silver platter. He took one glance at the crisp green fuck you and he burst into laughter.

Oscar was roaring. I was retelling an old war story.

"We threatened the life of an executive from the world's most popular arms manufacturing company and he thought it was funny. I mean Jesus! You threaten to kill a man and almost overnight The Bull became a culinary sensation."

"A critic sitting at an adjacent table said it was dish to die for. That was a bold review."

We finished our meals and eventually even consoled each other. I was very glad I got to see Oscar, but I was inevitably enticed back to my place by this rare gift.

The journal was wrapped up in a dirty red binding. I read my cousin's words and let the memories rush over me.

Malcolm's script was jotted down carefully, artfully recollecting the plot twists in the events of our lives. The words themselves were handled by pencil in a neat delicacy. I began to read what seemed like his final testament.

***

3/8/15:

"In memory, after I started getting paid, the cookbooks started stacking up around my place and were used as my dining room furniture and living room decor. Culinary tracts became end tables or cutting board platforms.

I collected old texts like *Liber de Coquina*, *The Forme of Cury*, *Larousse Gastronomique*, and Escoffier's works, all the way up to celebrity chef Marco Pierre White's *White Heat*. I'd go to the library to print out recipes from China and Japan. So much time was spent skulking down the internet's bizarre causeways just to find an ingredients list detailing the meals of Ottoman Sultans.

On top of work, staying up for days to scrapbook plans became a common occurrence. I needed to uncover the dietary requirements of Tibetan monks, Native American war chiefs, or just about any other son of a bitch who ever charred meat over an open flame.

Memorizing a recipe's intricacies was not enough. I needed to perform them. The theory was good, the practice gave it meaning.

I learned that through food you can unlock a historical vision of the past. It was usually clear what type of people were eating what food stuffs and whether the design stemmed from necessity or eccentricity. I read somewhere that

Khanate hordes nursed on blood from wounds pricked into their horses' necks. I read about how they'd stow mare's milk beneath their saddlebags and ride and churn the milk into cheese.

What did Tibetan monks subsist on? Did yak testicles have anything to do with enlightenment? When the testicles were grilled on a flat top, their gumminess released a fertile stench. I didn't like the taste but I could feel an austere power about eating them.

"Qu'ils mangent de la brioche!" Another fine example. Very well Marie Antoinette I will eat cake, and uncover the luxury baked into your downfall. Whether brioche or black bread, it became clear that you can understand a people's history through their cuisine. Secondarily, if you can shape the way people eat, you can shape the way they think.

All the way back, I could follow this loose chain of events throughout the constellations of human culture. Whether it be in that dreaded Spartan concoction of pig's legs, blood, salt and vinegar, or modernity's nervous nouveau riche compulsion to place a gold leaf on a chocolate sundae, eating became everything to me. I came to believe that our most earnest philosophy is found in the mouth, on the tongue, not with speaking but with eating.

At this point I memorized what seemed like thousands of recipes. It was not enough to simply know. For me knowledge is meant to be used to slice a swath unto desire itself.

Ultimately in the kitchen I learned that the body is the only honest philosopher."

9/27/18:

"What was The Brazen Bull to me?

It sounds strange but I had an impulse wash over me after driving home from a Martin McDonagh play.

His work is active and visceral. The stage blood splattered onto us. I was duly surprised by the work one man could accomplish in a world of his own. There's a power on the stage, the kitchen alike, where the playwright, the chef, could make his audience feel his fiction. And if he had a forceful enough willpower, he could transmute the imaginary into the sensory.

We were getting an offer from an investor friend to open up something a little further out west. After many years at Le Cheval I decided it was time.

I remember while I was doing research on Soviet recipes I found a quote from Vladimir Lenin of all people. At the preface of an 1927 Russian cookbook entitled: *Nutrition! The Engine of the Proletariat*, there was a quote stating "Every cook has to learn how to govern the state."

While the cookbook itself was none too fascinating, the idea resonated with me in my formative years when we were coming up with the idea of the restaurant as an edible theater. The idea was to fully allow others to leap tongue first into the imagination.

I knew artistic abilities have extraordinarily sincere physical effects. I needed to make those effects occur inside the dining room. My despotic drive was conjured in the same feeling I've been chasing my entire life. Manipulating the sensory in the world is fiction, is an act of sorcery.

At the soul root of my life's motivation, a certain drive for success took hold of me. I was always dangerously and intensely aware that we are all slipped for time. During the passion of creating I could feel a lessening of the mind's burden on the soul.

Cooking, or the culinary, whenever these words evolved, is the closest thing we have to the veritable artistic manipulation of life processes. In the materialist and metaphorical sense, I would have died If not for cooking. There was a decision somewhere along the way to honor that savior. I wanted to be the type of man to not only study the roots of human history through food, but to wield it and ration out my will-power into a perfectly cooked meal.

11/28/18:

"On opening night, from a one way window, I peered through a nook installed near the grill for me to gauge a client's reaction.

We served every steak to a ritualistic standard alluding to a borderline religious experience. Each filet we served was a natural orchestra on display.

I thanked God for his mercy in producing livestock for our humble earth. When I cooked meat for people I thought about the binding of Isaac, and Gabriel descending with a ram to prevent mankind from consuming itself.

As evident in history's most desperate situations, there is nothing to suggest that God's most desperate creature would not eat himself alive. Suppose with horror that suddenly no birds graced our vaulted skies. The food chain would collapse and our cornucopia of foods would be abolished into a withering globe of dust.

It's been indicated to me through my step-dad, through old biblical stories, that if man eats forbidden fruit, there is nothing to prevent him too from tasting forbidden flesh.

Deuteronomy 28:53, says "And thou shalt eat the fruit of thine own body, the flesh of thy sons and of thy daughters, which the Lord thy God hath given thee..."

What I mean is even outside of times of extreme hardship, human beings have a tendency to cannibalize. So with grace I take caution in our ability to eat at the expense of another; one who feels pain, and sorrow, one who feels love and happiness. If you did not raise animals you wouldn't know. And this is all so difficult to explain when it was my cow Apricot, whose newborn I raised, whose eventual death I enamored in the surahs I sung, and ultimately whose tenderloin I aimed to prepare, was all building a wicker statue for the burning up in a lifelong cacophony of emotion.

Cooking, beginning with birth, transforming into food through death, and being eaten to fuel my own existence, are all events in this larger conglomerate cycle. There was no difference for me in Om and the knocking of butcher's blades through bone. One thing that set The Brazen Bull apart as a restaurant was my direct connection to every piece of meat that was served.

I personally raised and killed everything."

***

2/10/19:

"After the Antonovka Apple Incident, I was left wondering how far a meal go.

That was the pivotal question. From there, I strayed from the wishes of my staff, advising against career implosion. From there I only upped the ante. My restaurant became an amphitheater to plot malicious performances.

My thoughts went back to one of our most extreme services. A modified Julia Child's Beef Burgundy with magic mushrooms. Our client that night was none other than Harry Manstein, the world famous rapist/film producer.

We served him, primarily because no other restaurant in Pittsburgh wanted the heat while Manstein was under investigation for nearly 90 rape allegations. By this point we were no stranger to controversy ourselves.

Manstein really was an ugly son of a bitch. Yet I greeted the bastard at the door with a smile. He signed waiver after waiver as we jumped through the law's fiery hoops. Thankfully my reputation's weight pulled the right heart strings and he was charmed into dining with us.

Our guest was the perfect recipient for this dish. His steady history of drug abuse was well known, so I was positive he would receive it in chaotically amusing taste.

We served the meal in a comfortable environment. The atmosphere and the meal were both so carefully devised as to set a precedent for comfortable monotony.

There was house-made bread and butter, well seasoned veg, our red wine, all selected as to not overly excite the palette. I sat through a simulation of the meal beforehand to sample the environment. The design was planned to be a five out of ten. Absolutely ahistorical, pristine in its capacity to be forgotten.

The temperature in the room was suburban. The water was issued from the city tap. Every element was devised to make you forget about struggle. No pain. No sacrifice.

Every ingredient was situated between a complaint and a compliment. I thought about fine dining under the auspices of the Clinton administration. The end of history. The roasted carrots tasted like pre-9/11 complimentary airplane food. I wanted go one further. We were culinary terrorists ready to take flight.

Manstein was expecting the meal of a lifetime, and out comes a Caesar salad. I had to contain myself. If I burst out into laughter he would know something was up. The first dosage of magic mushrooms was in the dressing. Slightly bitter. He ate it just fine. Bread and butter. My client was was sinking into primal astonishment. If you think something's wrong it's because it is Mr.

Manstein.

As the drug trip began so did our subtle alterations of decor. In the fireplace, the maitre d' dropped color altering chemicals. The dining room corner would occasionally burst into a violet, turning rosy posy, then to green.

During the wine tasting we applied a second dosage. Next step: add or remove furniture. If he asked why the paisley linen napkins lava-lamped in his lap, we would never acknowledge any difference.

"How long have I been here?" He asked.

The waiter replied according to script.

"Mr. Manstein you've always been here."

Sprinkle in a quote from *The Shining* to get under his skin. Applied Stasi torture techniques eroded his dinner experience from middle class comfort into a steady decomposition of reality. I remember at one point we were literally gas-lighting him, as the table side meal lamp flickered and dimmed.

Step three: switch waiters. Manstein looked at our young waiter Erik and asked, "Are the lights okay?"

Of course they are, they were always flickering like that. He was beginning to look like someone was trying to destroy him.

When Erik came back with the main course, he was not the same auburn haired young gentleman. He was now elderly and decrepit. Thankfully, our saucier Shannon knew a make up artist who was able to make Erik look like he aged 50 years in ten minutes.

The grand finale was to spill advocaat liqueur on our client after he'd finished up the main course. It was a rough set up but we had to take Manstein to a red-lit bathroom to wipe off the digestif, then quickly rearrange the entire dining room setting.

Rip down the wall paper, alter the table from oak to cherry, change the background music, place a photoshopped image of Manstein sitting at the rearranged dining room, just like in Kubrick's film, and serve vanilla ice cream for desert. We knew hardest part would be to maintain illusory monotony.

He came back to an utterly changed room while he was peaking on a high mushroom dosage. By this time he was seated to his boring ice cream dish. We cued Shannon's role as a battered naked actress to come out of the kitchen in bloody body paint. She crept up on him just like the decaying corpse from Room 227.

Forgive me please, it was Halloween. Lo and behold, Mr. Manstein stormed out to the sound of my laughter. I couldn't help it! We were all trapped in The Brazen Bull together.

Headlines were sure to be made. And in retrospect, they were inevitable. Psychedelic haunted house was not my most disciplined culinary endeavor, but it is also said we eat with our eyes first."

***

I paled over my Malcolm's writings as I laid down on my cold bedroom mattress, milling my mind over what Malcolm believed was motivating him, wondering where exactly things began to go wrong. What ideas fed his brain, and lead up to the point where he snapped?

Where in the play he was narrating for himself was it written that every event had to come to one decisive conclusion? And ultimately what justified murder?

I puzzled myself into an inconclusive, though all interlocking mandala of events where human pieces formulate a concise rhythm of acts. The overall image eluded me.

I fell asleep knowing that I was going to drive to the farm tomorrow. I am going to stand at the location where Malcolm made his last stand and contrive some sort of answer for myself. I will find out why my cousin felt that it was time for him to relinquish his life.

I drove into Malcolm's Farm and I pulled into the driveway where the police blew him away. Journal in hand, I walked up to his old front porch and I sat down where he died and read the final entry.

He detailed the last day of his existence with metronome precision.

***

1/9/21:

"I was about to take a brief hiatus for the season but I promised a client one last meal.

We were going to sacrifice Taurus for our best beef dish yet. No tricks either. It was going to be straightforward. We were going to put aside shock value, hide the irony, put the references in the closet, and steep ourselves in our craft.

Hans Bloomqvist, a Swedish food magazine editor and one of our most fierce critics, was our final guest. Since our doors opened Bloomqvist needed to test our mettle, mostly because he was an advocate for cruelty free cooking. I was always happy to oblige anyone.

It began innocently enough as a stand off between our two perspectives. Bloomqvist had just about switched over to complete veganism, and I was well known for my meticulous treatment of flesh for food. The wager was that I could switch a "cruelty free" individual back to an omnivore in the space of a meal. The idea fascinated me so I took it in stride.

Hans Bloomqvist came to Pittsburgh on January 9th and I even sent for a taxi service to pick him up.

Our esteemed guest possessed an upright stature and strong brows which cupped green eyes. His chest betrayed the stereotype of gay effeminacy. There was nothing effeminate about him despite the constant image placating about a limp-wristed vegan. When he walked in through the doors of The Brazen Bull, I saw absolutely no indicator of malnourishment. In fact, Bloomqvist looked like he was raised on the fat of the land. Maybe he was a liar?

I saw him and he seemed overall very uncritical. He lacked the hunched reserve of many miserable food critics who write their legacies into slander pieces designed to cry for personal attention.

Regrettably, both my future and my past were determined by food psychologists.

These people were writing their biographies and paying the bills with my art. These dickheads and pussies were all trying to trounce around the Freudian undertones in my food, or a feminist logic à la Beauvoir, or looking for a post-colonial interpretation on dining colorism. They could all go fuck themselves as far as I was concerned.

It's because of them I developed an an immediate distrust for psychological people overall. They swim in their own shit. I begged their miserable intellects to distance themselves from me, if they must muddy the waters in order to seem deep. They're misanthropes. But they taught me one lesson: Misery is occasionally a choice.

After my third Michelin star, the heft of my own legacy's ball and chain became as nebulous to me as mercury. What else could anyone teach me? But still Bloomqvist was different, he looked like he didn't need psychology.

My only concern at the time was Bloomqvist's recently adopted militancy. Hans and his followers would barricade the gates of cattle farms wherever he would go. As Hans toured the globe ransacking local businesses of their supplies, he would send out messages ahead of time telling local activists where to meet up. Why would my restaurant be anything other than an opportunity to protest the eating of meat? I had faith. I thought he would be different, so I treated him differently.

As I personally seated the food critic, I chided him into following my customs. I had a contractual obligation to serve beautiful food to all of my clients, to provide them with a meal, and in return I expected two very simple things: provide payment and respect.

The first is obvious, the second should be intuitive. Do not insult my staff and do not befoul the meal of another guest or your own. If that is all said and very easily done you can expect an experience backed by my personal honor.

The plan was simple. I bring out a several portions of my best steak. He tastes it, and writes an honest review. I put my reputation on the line, and he stakes his morals. At least it should've been that simple.

For this reason I slaughtered my prize calf. I remember Taurus, my precious baby bull, who I helped nourish and raise. My time with him was delightful, though killing Taurus was another matter.

The night before Bloomqvist arrived I seized the little calf from the barn. His breath bounced in panic, heaving operatic squeals to his mother and over to the other animals who know the scent of slaughter. It was absolutely necessarily that he was killed according to scripture.

After walking up to the barn door, a nursing bull calf went with me around the barn door side and into a separate wooden structure. I gave him grain, and fresh water, and caressed him. Quickly I clenched his mouth shut and took him up by the hooves.

Bismillahir Raḥmānir Raḥīm

The knife sharpened for prayer's swift incision, slit past the jugular and the wind pipe and carotid. The ululating creature whimpered pitifully. Then took to bucking bravely like a bull grown well past his age.

His brown fur, sleek, wet at the neck, grew blacker against his ruby red interior. He thrashed about widening a gaping wound, yelping from a second mouth. Slowly, his fitful eyes began to glaze over, narrowing as if looking into brightness, or on into the infinity of infinities. And with that Taurus transformed into veal for tomorrow's supper.

I analyzed the supple meat, cloudy with fat. Looking carefully, I saw how his underdeveloped muscles were draped in pearly fat ribbons curled around warm bone.

I took the veal inside and salted it and stored all but several strips of it in the kitchen fridge for dry brining.

For myself, I put a stainless steel frying pan over the gas stove to prepare the recently slain calf. On the stainless steel the veal took a sear in olive oil. I basted the cut with butter made from his mother's milk.

Cooking at this level was the turning of tragic truth into an emblem of delicacy.

The beef darkened to the color of crusty brown soil melting into one congruent rich morsel. The scent was indeed delicate, but in a way where I was not sure if I was salivating or about to be sick. This emotion confused me. The temptation to eat swayed me in and out of wolfishness, then like a pendulum back into guilt.

I was all consumed by that little calf, who's yearling body coddled balmy sunlight. I remember the way his dark eye delighted in the tawny blossoms and the way he came to me when I called. I glanced out at the barn. Imagining his mother's udders swelling with pressure, her underside strangely cold, fully stunted by agonizing confusion. Though I must say once more the aroma wafts and I am ravenous.

The next day was solemn.

With Hans seated, I placed a thin filet with several tasting salts, at the base of a wooden chopping board. We made direct eye contact as I pressed my first knife into the filet, cutting thin slices.

"This was the knife I used to slaughter tonight's meal."

He looked carefully at the portions. I hoped he would delve into the origins of the cooking process and see what I saw.

His right hand came up to the table settings, feeling the edge of the cutting board I used to serve our guest. I didn't realize what he intended to do. I watched Hans Bloomqvist slide the religiously prepared meal off the table and onto the ground. The steak hit the carpet.

Without thinking, I reached for my chef's knife, the same one first given to me at Le Cheval by my first mentor and I plunged it into into the chest of Hans Bloomqvist.

The knife's sabre-like steel had broken off into Bloomqvist's body. The knife was destroyed. It served its purpose.

Bismillahir Raḥmānir Raḥīm

I looked my staff who stood wordless, and at my clients who'd witnessed a murder. I broke my own rules. I befouled my guests' meals. I didn't know what to do so I walked out the front door. I got in my car and I drove home.

East on 376, I was nearly back at my farm.

On the hills a storm turned furiously.

A flash of lighting ripped through black clouds on the barren mountains and a cataclysmic lightingscape blinked over the naked hills and the jagged bough shaped bolts made aplomb turns towards torrid death.

After another 15 minute drive I pulled into my land and parked in my orchard. I walked and waded into the unbecoming browns where the tree trunks' colors sank into a drab mixture.

The sky was a muddy oil painting and the artist splattered dusk colors liberally.

I slogged through ground daubed by hay for my animals near the drinking pond. A text message from my sous-chef Henri said the food critic lost two liters of blood. He was not gonna make it. It was a shame that perfectly good flesh went to waste. Then again, the animal I slaughtered for him was drained of so much more. Body and spirit. Not like it meant anything to him. Not like he was using it.

I thought about recipes some more, about standing my ground. I knew the cops would probably come soon.

Evening. Approaching. Evening in the lyrical tense. Nectarine assumed its expressive hotness jettisoning its quick-light over a worldly solarium. The sunset scalded hard. It was a sunset so declarative, so ancient, and so worshipful, that it must have stunned us spiritually even before man became contemplative in his God. Reds and blues snared the valleyed hills and for some reason I thought of the Symphony No. 7 Op. 92. The cop cars were coming with a vengeful seriousness that filled me with a light bounty.

This story could end here.

Another nut job snagged himself on the wrong end of the law. Maybe I was fucked since the beginning. Police sirens were getting closer and with my last meal under wraps, I figured I might as well do the dishes for the crime scene cleanup crew. That would make me a good host when they scrub me off the hardwood. I've always heard about morbidity as something adjacent to kitchen sink realism.

Psychologists mention a macabre contrast between a severed hand being stored next to the Reeses' cups in the serial killer's freezer.

Over the valley farmland, clouds and their runaway horses spanned the mountainous overlooks. I studied my heart, finding a vivid pulse and a deep breath. They were stern inhales of air in between each deep draw. Each exhalation was comfortably final. The shrill sirens closed in, sounding off like a bomb shelter warning you of the end of the world. Correction: the end of the world for me.

I sat down on the wooden stoop of my porch. My cousin Ryan once told me that a life is worth the entire world. So I wondered what I was trading it all in for. I was working in the currency of air, and each transaction was duly secured in advance by the metabolism. Both the body and its parts are in a continuous state of dissolution and nourishment, so they are inevitably undergoing permanent change.

The body says, "There is the feeling of being alive, and then there is not. What else is there to be concerned with?" So in this creeping instance, I was trading in the world for my dignity.

The critic I slaughtered used counterfeit breath to pay for deathless lifetimes. I wasn't so desperate. I resolve to say that there are things worth relinquishing, life included. You can only handle so much dishonor. And if I went peacefully with the police, I will be locked in a cage and that will be that. Such a fate would go against my principles, knowing full well that they wouldn't let me cook in jail.

Cop cars were pulling into my extended drive way near the orchard. I am seeing flashing lights and hearing the sirens and I seeing back to earlier times. Before I opened The Brazen Bull, before the Michelin stars, before Bloomqvist, before junk habits.

The cops are exiting their vehicles. I can't avoid the dreamlike feeling that I was revisiting old choices made at crucial turning points. It seems that despite countless opportunities to redefine every decision I've ever mismade, there was no going back. There is no surrender. I am set on a faithful path. This is my life. This is the ending I've selected for it. This is where I want my story to end. My mind stuffed my life into a VCR, and pressed rewind."

***

That was it.

I closed the notebook, and sat down on his old front porch. The dreaminess of life transmuting every day events into effervescence washed over me. I laid down on the front porch, trying to synthesize his impulses into sensical decisions. I want to find something radically meaningful in it, to lurch around for a martyr where one couldn't be made. For the rest of my life I will be left to suppose my relative, "the genius", died antithetically to a definitive plot-line. He left us all on an unresolvable cliff hanger.

As I laid back on the porch, leaning into oblivion, I learned it's not enough to become a martyr. Today, it's not a victory to die for one's cause and it's not enough to destroy oneself or one's opposition. What am I trying to say?

Sometimes an impulse is just an impulse and the crazy are simply insane.

The Assassination Marketplace

A character is a completely fashioned will. - Novalis

It was the 23rd. The night before Christmas Eve.

Snow blew out of a dormant twilight. Main Street turned white and the snow lent itself to the tips of disappearing tree tops and the white lent itself to the poetry of Christina Rosetti.

The wind speaking in whispers in the bleak midwinter was a living Christmas poem and the white had a transitory effect of making poetic objects completely disappear.

Out of shop windows, cream colored lights gleamed upon flecks of affected snow and pristine particles of ice flickered upon every other clover in the grass. At night, the sleep-like snow blanketed all things living and unliving. In the winter of 2020 even history itself seemed to be asleep; perhaps it was just on sabbatical.

Ari Alekhine was walking along with his hands in his long-coat pockets. He was crunching the snow beneath his boots.

Christmastime came with its everyday grandeur. His step had a joyful loftiness to it. He saw holiday lights accosting people with a happy beauty. He looked up from the sidewalk and caught a glimpse of a large Hotel Bethlehem sign's invariable radiance. The red neon was magnified by the glimmering of snow falling upon snow.

Maria was walking down the road a little towards his way. She stretched her left eye wide to playfully emulate Ari's own misshapen pupil. She liked to remind him of his eye's dogged grayness; from an infantile wound he'd received when the delivery nurse dropped him on his head.

His mother loved to tell the story about how her baby's placenta slicked heel slipped through the nurse's glove the day he was born.

Ari entered the world very quietly. It happens occasionally. Stillbirth makes men wonder why God puts lives on earth already accomplished. Babies get born. They're only given a couple minutes. That's how it goes. But when gravity first bore down on Ari's fleshy body, his own weight was heavy enough to snap the umbilical chord.

After he hit the ground, the newborn started to cry. Ari's mother screamed at the nurse to pick him up. In her arms her son's fingers fluttered at consciousness. It took a moment for his soul to assume its vessel.

She stared at her baby in awe; his soul feeling the contours of its body for the first time. One can't help but imagine a newborn baby's sensory overload; experiencing its maniacal mind blossoming into its body all at once. Sound, touch, taste, sight, smell. Everything for first time.

As he got older his eyes developed uncomfortably. His skewed vision caused extreme sensitivity to sunlight so he stayed inside most of the day and up until late at night.

Despite Ari's disfigurement, his mother saw a peculiar beauty in the results. The pair of eyes became as mismatched as Neptune and Pluto. The right pupil hardened into a dense sapphire, while the other developed off kilter; not quite planetary.

All throughout his life, Ari's left eye floated around like an unfortunate asteroid orbiting the other eye serving to enhance the adjacent sapphire's asterial blue.

Maria kissed him and she took him by the arm.

The couple didn't struggle terribly for money, though it was not plentiful. Maria was a committed schoolteacher and Ari rarely escaped the hermitage of a bedroom afforded to him by a fledgling writing career. When time afforded they spent all of their time going on walks or cooking dinner with one together. When they walked or went to go meet acquaintances, Maria lead the walking and did the talking while her hair made way for the couple.

In any weather her head was fully composed of red-orange locks, bob cut just above her eyebrows. Her eyes played pinball in her head, collecting data to churn out 10,000 thoughts per minute. This well oiled machine was perpetually overheated beneath coils of hot copper wire, but never burnt out of words or stories. She was a woman of essences, and he uncovered them one by one on their first dates.

He realized after their first meeting in the spring of 2018, she converted everyday existence into one immaculate obstruction. Love became an extremity, a road block, an abrupt end to avoiding the world as a simple externality. Before he met Maria he had never considered the natural scent of a woman; beforehand a woman's scent was only conceived in manufactured femininity.

They were attending a Christmas party. Alekhine's latest novel, *The Assassination Marketplace*, was a topic of conversation. This 186 page book told the story of a disgruntled liberal turned anarchist who plotted revenge on Jeffery Epstein's fictional political colleagues. These fictional colleagues fell victim to a dark web conspiracy in which an alter-ego masterminded the construction of a malevolent crowdfunding campaign.

In this hypothetical historical retelling, Americans nationwide could elect a hit upon one of their own villainous elite. Not unlike a political action committee, cryptocurrency users could elect an assassination with their own funds to make their voices heard.

Had *The Assassination Marketplace* remained a simple story Alekhine would've never been described in a *Wall Street Journal* article as "the vicious lovechild of Steve Jobs and Gavrilo Princip."

Another newspaper sideline Ari enjoyed came from a *Washington Post* op-ed entitled, "Elon Musk meets Robespierre: DIY Anarchism and Crowdfunding the Reign of Terror." In this article a journalist detailed The Assassination Marketplace's ability to merge revolutionary fervor with the slacktivist ethos.

After The Assassination Marketplace many Americans came to assume that there was no difference between bullet ballistics and political science. Just to think this could've all remained safe within a book.

The midnight of Christmas Eve, Ari took Maria into a side room to get away from the party and held her close to him. He said that he was getting a headache and was going outside to get some fresh air.

That was the last she would see of him in person.

***

That was all Miss Maria Roy would confess during her interrogation and I have no reason to believe she knew anything otherwise.

About a year since unbridled levels of political instability, it'd never been officially declared if Alekhine was behind his own plot or not. And if he was well… that would never be *officially* reported to me.

But I knew the reality.

Everyone *knew.*

Alekhine was at the very bare minimum the inspiration behind website because he wrote the idea for it of course.

It was never for certain whether or not he was the one who turned his inspiration into a reality.

"All he did was write a book." Miss Roy said.

As far as the evidence is concerned, this is true.

Naturally her deceased boyfriend was the number one suspect, the only suspect for that matter. We had every reason withholding the lack of demonstrable proof to suspect that Ari Alekhine's activism wasn't merely confined within the borders of a mediocre novel. His mother told us everything she knew and gave us free rein to search every nook in her apartment.

Still we found nothing to suggest that Alekhine had even authored a website, or financed any malicious networks, or set up a terrorist assassination infrastructure. In fact there was no proof that he was even paying an internet bill.

While we had no reason to suspect he was acting alone, the FBI agents handling the case always believed he had made some tangible contribution to crowdfunding high profile killings. More interestingly, there is an entire conspiracy surrounding Alekhine's murder.

Many more unanswered questions. If the architect of The Assassination Marketplace was someone inspired by the text, who was reading it? We found no illicit connections with any customers.

Also, who was responsible for Alekhine's death and why was he killed? These questions became the conversation of just about every tuned in person in the country. Spiritually, it was part two of the Jeffrey Epstein scandal.

There were conspiracies upon conspiracies surrounding motives from within the "political elite", or the CIA or the "deep state" of course. Some believed that right wing nationalists were trying to preserve the integrity of the Republic by killing Alekhine. Others thought there was an coup d'etat underway to destroy the networks of power. Nobody could know in the end because he never got to stand trial.

On the shelf just above my fire place I picked up a ratty paperback and turned to a random page. I read.

"The Assassination Marketplace will be our attempt to hold the power players accountable. Isn't that a democratic issue? Lack of punishment for lack of accountability? Who would get in trouble if you could disperse blame so thin that no one person could possibly take ownership of the catastrophe? It's direct democracy, but for permanently weeding out corrupt elements."

He says it right there in not so fictional terms.

That's a hell of a thing to write. Can you charge a guy with hundreds of counts of conspiracy to commit first degree murder because he wrote it in a book?

Higher ups in the State Department had gotten involved despite the fact that Ari had no criminal background to speak of.

In high school he was described by his peers as sociable. He maintained very high grades and played tennis. He was bookish, and fascinated by computer coding. Harmless was the condensed version of his personality.

That would be all well and good if The Assassination Marketplace did not create a nation wide crisis resulting in no one wanting to run for state level office.

I flipped the pages from his journal in my living room while I debated the flames-worth of several same such journals, containing air headed idealisms. As the fireplace coals eked out a meager existence, I was sifting through his whole self-recorded life for any signs of illicit connections between crypto wallets, extremist militancy, or terror organizations. In the end I was only finding philosophical mockeries. They were almost directed my way. Insulting me, laughing about how Ari was my opposite. And the more I read them, the more I thought the journals beckoned to be burned. They wanted to be spent as chronicles made calories.

I stood by an open window letting cool air enter the room to further entropy. Outside, water droplets hitting the tilted glass panes burst into the sound of rain reading itself.

I heard from his lawyer that Ari wanted to make it clear in court that his idea began as an essay, an experiment if you will, to test the creative limits of free speech. Too bad for him, Alekhine never made it past the third circuit steps.

Despite being largely unsuccessful as a writer, *The Assassination Marketplace* brought an allowance of fear into the hearts of its few readers. For a period of two weeks Alekhine was the most wanted man in America. And when the FBI caught him they were semi-shocked at the self-awareness of who we all assumed to be the Marketplace's founder. Not quite the Oppenheimer we were looking for, nor the Gavrilo Princip, had he known his actions would've lead to World War I.

Alekhine indicated no remorse. Is that because he couldn't care about a crime he didn't commit?

I put down his book and flipped to a random journal entry. This entry contained the details that were cited as the confirmation of his unprovable guilt.

Ari writes, "Ironically as I saw to the lessening of my prospects, I began to see a logic in the high wire. We are raised to assume a demonstrable reality, to walk down tunnels leading to mediocre places bored for us by boring people. Mediocrity knows he's a clever bastard. He's a best friend, an accountant of days, who leads you to your daily allotment of comfort. All the while his warm smile covers a front so fraud can slip in through the back.

People thought I was an insane person because I saw absolutely no reason why I should not be delusionally optimistic.

It's the case that realistic sensibilities have only lead me to realistic expectations. When you finally settle for anything life becomes very long and very comfortable. In and out and in and out. Imagine a kingdom built in purgatory where even an orgasm becomes routine. The less you have, the less you have to lose, the less you are weighed down.

The purity of The Assassination Marketplace is in its delusional optimism. It was a drive for liberty masked by a love for humanity. Can I say that I get sick and tired of eating it? I was reading the other night about how the Hindu goddess Kali demonstrates her garland strung with freshly severed heads and in doing so wields the ugliness required to spur change. I must exercise this force. - May 24th, 2020"

I shut the journal.

I can remember holding him as he died on the concrete steps outside the James A. Byrne Courthouse in Philadelphia.

Out of a crowd, reporters dashed towards us, falsely shielding us in light thrown by many a camera's sniping flash. Out of a police car and up the courthouse steps officers hauled a drab jumpsuit. He scowled at them and then a bleak thunder struck the block. He dropped. A bullet burrowed through his brain and tore into weak webs of grey matter. A bullet hole left his mind splayed out in a defecate mound on the concrete behind his bleeding head.

I watched the young Alekhine's spirit leave his body through a blown out emergency exit. After pressing into the hot cavity underneath his mismatched eyes, his fully vanquished spirit left his skull a shallow place.

I kept looking, they were shaking the lifeless head. Behind his sockets there was nothing, less than nothing, a nudity beneath bones. We were hauling him towards the sidewalk where my fingers touched blast blanched skin, caressing an exit wound.

His right eye was completely drained. It still held its power; a perfect reflection of the sky, a negative beauty, a mystical gem capable of entrancing every subject it inhabits. My vise grip on his life slipped away into a pristine and airy nothingness, into life beyond limit-experience. I saw Ari's arms transform into simple body parts. There I was on the sidewalk, face to face with the irreparable truth in witnessing a human being become simple material.

Returning to his journals I still couldn't bring myself to destroy them. Though I must. I am supposed to destroy them as to not incriminate myself in evidence theft.

The fire's fading fury gave me more of an excuse to preserve their words.

Another notebook opened. I paged through it. A notebook snapped shut at the spine.

Before he died, I thought I was going to keep his project afloat for as long as realistically possible. I hoped that things would get shaken up and people would feel secure in their vengeance. That was the point after all.

On the inside, with as much cryptographic experience as anyone in the State Department need have, I was able to keep the Marketplace afloat. It is because of me that Ari Alekhine managed his endeavors for as long as he did, and he was lucky that someone very high up felt his kindred guilt. Though if I kept him alive too long it would become suspicious.

With immense sadness, I paid a large amount money to have him murdered, and he was dead because his invention operated with a 95% success rate which plunged the public and private sectors into chaos.

The rain stopped.

Standing at the fireplace I was preparing to burn the memoirs of someone who I hated and loved at the same time. He reminded me of my own soured hopes. He showed me an origin of loathing, stemming from a toxic substance that once invigorated me.

Ari had something to say for a moment like this.

He writes, "I'm going to be brutally honest, this whole project is gleaned from a single solitary hope that I might finally pay the ransom of my dreams. These dreams ambushed me in all shapes and exerted their force upon me. I looked directly above my desk where I dreamt where there was a white spider galloping across my ceiling like a tiny pale horse.

At my writing desk I was getting good at splitting my psyche in two; at negotiating my time in between reality and a world that is infinite. In the attic just above my room, I knew there was a nest of them.

At first the spider's nest unnerved me. Then anxiety surrendered to wonder which all gave way to immaculate subtlety.

It was the same subtlety found in fear turned fascination, like lightning tearing into a night sky's jacquard. People would see my eyes and believe that I was possessed by a monster, but Maria saw something magisterial in me.

I learned that spiders possess all the qualities of little angels, God's many eyed translucent friends. I can remember one spider in particular with its wispy wings. The spider approached me by way of a long descent from the ceiling. Gliding down on a silver strand it floated downwards inch by inch, unraveling its iridescent spools.

Sitting back into my chair I was fully bewildered by this living metaphor for audacity, drifting around my face, weaving our fate into gossamer.

When the spider finally reached me at nose level. Its silk unfurled for what would be miles in comparison to the size of the insect. He turned to me and we looked at each other. There was no guarantee I would not crush him. For a moment the spider remained still. After our long pause he returned to his task. His effortless journey was the climbing of insane heights.

My hope was that I could do something to leave an everlasting impression on someone."

And I stopped there because I felt a sorry sickness in my stomach. It is the disgust that comes with the decadence of failed idealism.

For our own sake I made the decision that there will be no more destiny. There doesn't need to be any evidence of that type of naivety. Hopeful idealisms should not be making an impact upon our society.

The journal pages took flame.

But I kept one snippet for myself.

That night when I went to bed I could hear him reading it to me.

His insane writings are the syllables rhythmically drifting me into sleep; thoughts upon thoughts disappearing as quietly as the sound of melting snow.

I remember his final written words.

> *I am living the lie,*
> *That if enough is done,*
> *I shall not die.*

The Shimamura Incident

"Many men are not born. They are manufactured. They might become men, but are made artificial."

My vision was locked into a dying ember draining ash from an incense tower. He was looking out of the window with his eyes lurching up towards an indigo lakeland.

A 3D printer howled like a banshee in the corner of the one room apartment. In strands, hot plastic rendered the bone pale frame of a machine developing a machine developing a machine. We were waiting for the next stage of history. The future smelled like burning plastic. The countryside rich in animal shit fought against the future.

I asked him what he meant by that.

"Conceptually I knew they would take two years of my life. You arrange the math every which way when you're about to serve a prison sentence. And what formula tortured me the most was the fact that it was two summers, two winters, two springs and falls of my life, all billed to a cage."

As he was speaking, the young man sitting across from me had an unsuspicious look about him. I couldn't recognize anything criminal about his outward appearance, a fault of mine which the Kyoto police had no problem overcoming. If he looked like he could be someone's dad, that's because he was.

Shimamura said no pictures and no recordings.

To my own embarrassment the whole interview was conducted in one language because his English was nearly as good as my own. During a conversational test-run my Japanese shivered.

"If you want to hear about a true crime, my girl was nine months pregnant and she gave birth the night I got put away. In Kyoto, where we were living, my sister contacted me in the evening saying that Mizuki was going into labor. She told me that cops were waiting for me outside of the emergency room. They knew where to look. Yukiko told me Mizuki was preparing to give birth on the seventh floor. The room had a window. Believe it or not I had to sneak up into the oncology ward and watch Mizuki give birth to my child from a building across the street."

Shimamura lowered his gaze and pinched the pale skin in between his brow. The somber story climaxed with his vision of his baby's blood burnished crown. He described to me in detail how a human baby bloomed from his girlfriend's womb. I'll never forget his face as he described his newborn daughter sipping air, the coldness of her first breath stunning her little lungs.

He said, "I was crying, and at first tears were flooding the view through my binoculars. At that moment a nurse came into the room and I had to hide the binoculars under my coat. He thought I heard bad news. Poor guy was hugging me because he thought I had been diagnosed with cancer, and part of me felt like that was true."

Shimamura started laughing while he torched a cigarette, adding to the myriad of smells crowding the room.

"And then after that you went to prison?"

My question shifted his emotion. He looked out of his curtains. It reminded me of that famous photo of Malcolm X, holding a rifle, prepared to defend his home to the death.

"Not immediately." He looked back at me with a paranoid glare. "I had a gift prepared for our baby because I knew Mizuki would be going into labor at any moment."

Shimamura recalled driving home with one last thing to do.

He could remember his truck tires churning through a tricolored deluge, the crimson rain droplets splitting hard, briefly bouncing up on the road like wheat fields, regenerating into protean blades of grass.

"I pulled up to our home very carefully, without a second thought of how quickly risk had lost its grim patina. There on the porch I left a plush lamb, a gift from her father, which would be my daughter's first worldly possession. You can't imagine my reluctance when I sat down on the stoop and called the police on myself. Court was quick and I plead guilty to expedite a surprisingly light sentence of only two years, or 730 days, or 17,520 hours. My only hope at the time was to get home before my daughter had any recollection of me being gone."

Shimamura turned to the machine. Watching a 3D printer create an object is like nothing you've ever seen before. A weapon spaghettified out of pure math into wax and collected articulately on a printing tray.

"It's like a hot glue gun." I said.

He nodded.

The first piece was coming together. The pistol barrel was oddly shaped though efficiently produced. He stood up to shuck the thumb sized cylinder off the printing platform and launched it hot potato at me. I looked through a bullet sized peephole at its creator, who leaned over his laptop spamming orders.

The 3D printer came back to life.

"Did you ever go to jail before Andrew?" He asked me.

"Do I look like it?"

"I can't say so, but neither do a lot of people."

The printer began churning out the next firearm part.

He continued. "I didn't even know at the time that it was illegal to print guns. But I don't think anyone did. It's a strange feeling going to prison for something nobody knew was possible."

He sat back down. There was a brief lull in the conversation. Shimamura didn't like talking about jail so he had to gather himself for the questions I didn't have the nerve to ask.

"My cell had a little window to the outside world. From one porthole foodstuffs were delivered to my cell by guards. On the opposite side my true nourishment was delivered."

Shimamura tried to describe the plexiglass from which he went window shopping for shimmering jewels.

"A malnourished cat might scurry by to lay its tongue upon a morsel of food left from my dinner. Sometimes a songbird might land on the concrete outcropping. I'd listen for laughing school children walking by the prison in the morning. All the details I collected contained worlds full of memories that helped me escape monotony induced dementia. And all these little gems became further fuel for dreams. Sadly I got very good at dreaming. In prison there was an acrid cagey stench meshed into every vision and my mattress became a derelict vehicle piloted by sleep."

Shimamura described his experience in earnest detail.

"I felt the next two years of life, a streamline of events, slipping away into an already abandoned future."

He put out his cigarette.

"One day I thought fuck it. I'm just gonna kill myself. Not for some *seven lives for my country* nonsense. This wasn't political anymore. I didn't believe in that. I didn't care about my country or human rights, or for any of the theory that I once impassioned myself with. Even less, I couldn't be bothered to go on as a scapegoat. I didn't even care about guns anymore or other people. The cynical part in me thought people didn't deserve them anyway."

"It's sad to hear you say that because the gun printers lauded you. They said you performed your work without fear or dishonor. But you make it seem like the sacrifice was totally in vain."

As I finished my sentence, a contemplative smirk dialed up his ears.

"The really funny thing is I learned more about freedom from inside of a cell than I ever could've anywhere else in the world."

He paused to check on the printer.

"At my most idealistic I always believed that human beings did not need to be taught the meaning of freedom. I saw the firearm as an opportunity for radical equality. Quite simply, the firearm as a humanism. I believed that because the human being is too precious to be left undefended."

"A lot of people saw you as selfish, putting your politics before the safety of others. You were treated like a terrorist. Like you were already an assailant." I said.

"Yes I've heard that a thousand times before. What we don't realize is that freedom itself is selfish. I saw the way I used the internet and I realized it was a mirror of who I really am. The way I see it, your search history is a history of you searching for who you really are. And sure one day someone will get killed by a 3D printed gun, it could even be me. I don't care because it hasn't happened yet but it will soon."

He picked up the bench scraper and chiseled off the Liberator's pistol grip from another printer.

"Of course there was a time during my sentence where I wished I never gave birth to the zig zag revolver and that I could've spent time with my daughter. Naturally these are all selfish thoughts."

He took a breath and continued.

"When I wasn't thinking about killing myself I was thinking about my daughter. At the time of my little epiphany it'd been exactly one full year since I'd last seen her, which made it her first birthday. And that whole day was spent agonizing over the value of my own life, staring at her precious face enshrined in a wallet sized portrait. From the lamp lit ceiling, hallowed light was shining through the transparent photo beatifying her. In that picture I'd never seen anything so righteous."

Shimamura started scratching off excess ABS plastic from the receiver to fit in with the trigger group.

"I realized that what I loved so much about my daughter is that she didn't ask to be born. Babies don't make requests, they make demands. Sitting in my cell I felt an ascetic rebellion stemming from the idea that existence possesses an instinctive will to creation. I began to weep vengefully with an immense satisfaction in the knowledge that not even God could undo my creation. That night the tears streamed down the side of my cheeks, dampening my pillow case."

Inspiration came laced with a cruel inflection distilled in his voice.

Shimamura spoke, "I did not ask to be born. Weak people always use that phrase as an excuse for their own shortcomings. Pardon the cliché but it is technically true. I know that I did not negotiate. I know some fall victim to their own bodies. I, on the other hand, took my life as captive. My daughter's birth reminded me how I instinctually leapt at the chance of a beating heart and how, in a nine month siege, my soul took my flesh prisoner."

I looked at the man in awe as he handed me the Liberator pistol, fully manufactured from extra parts made yesterday, a rubber band, and a nail used to strike a bullet's primer.

"I had my 'how' and if everything went according to plan I would be free in one year's time. No more jail. Only freedom. That's what I thought to myself. I figured that as long as I had my own reasons I never needed to die."

"So tomorrow we shoot the 3D printable firearm."

Shimamura grinned back at me.

It was early. The man glides pale and thin onto our makeshift range. We meet in a lush backwoods thirty minutes away from his home, quite out of the way. I watched Shimamura walk with a body purchased on borrowed time. I remember thinking to myself, "Was this one of the unsung bastards of history? This misfit who whistles a song as he throws caution to the wind. How many of him are there out there?"

An overpopulated worldful.

Shimamura brought two different guns in a briefcase. One was his own zig zag revolver design and the other was the liberator single-shot pistol we printed last night.

His zig zag snaps open.

The damned dusk broke quick by whipped horses hauling fright. The revolver's cylinder digests eight rounds, .22 LR, built to buck death subsonic. I took aim with the gun and fired west. The bullet claps through a line of percolating oak fronds. He didn't recommend a second firing.

On the other side of our makeshift firing range a Buddhist shrine laid tomblike, bombed out in the war, never repaired. In the deep woods, Shimamura told me old shrines out in the countryside were built to remind people that plants and animals are one and the same. I saw the exploded shrine and saw in it a ceaseless grind towards an atomless world.

Siddhartha was only partially correct. Shimamura, like Buddha, believed we will one day the world will become sound, an Om, a rhythm, an equation, a pulse, and then we would become *unregulated.*

Next the Liberator, a forerunner of its kind, flecked in a sinewy plastic musculature. In the sunlight it glowed white-gold.

Much of today's 3D printing is done by a process of additive manufacturing, a process by which language births plastic through electric synapses. The frame, the barrel, the trigger group, all fizzled out of thin air into solid concepts.

"In 3D printing we have a word. *Physible.* A stage basking between brain spasms, between conception and creation, between thought and action. *Physible*, means a file, a computer language, a set of pulsing signals begging to be born, to be made tangible. In these gun files, I saw an idea in its platonic potency, I saw its form, and then I saw a gun in my hand. Then at once many prosthetic limbs, guns, cars, sprinting through the ether from a raving shadowland. To me the 3D printer is an altar of unlimited information for which there is so much hope. From a single letter of code we could recreate the entire universe."

He spoke, and I believed every sound that came from his mouth.

It fired perfectly the first time. In reality, the Liberator might very well explode in your hand if you shoot it twice. I thought it ironic that the weapon itself, in practicality, was so useless but the potential for liberty, so immense. Magnificent.

Shortly afterwards, my excursion to visit Japan's first gun printer came to a close. I thanked Shimamura for the opportunity and we parted ways. It wasn't long after that I went back home to Pittsburgh.

Two weeks later, the article went out to a chorus of mild intrigue within the 3D printing community.

It was while I was on a walk overlooking the Allegheny that I stopped to look at the Pittsburgh skyline from a hillside promontory.

Already the world we knew was steadily rewriting itself into ones and zeroes; becoming a world burdened by so much information without origin.

The Allegheny River with its darkling gloss intimidated me. The sunlight made the river a road spanning infinity.

I knew now that they could never censor the firearm. No one could. My hope was that for the rest of time no one could strip life of its inherent danger, and that like Shimamura each one of us would become the usurpers of meaning. He helped me see that will power is measured in action. He showed me how the word made the world, and the intense capacity for world-making meaning is born from language. Speaking is very dangerous.

For the people who lament that they did not choose to be born, I wanted them to know that I chose the song of the world and that we are on two sides of the same coin.

Though, we are on a fringe. Change is coming. We will soon reach a tipping point, and we will soon have to decide how the future will be spoken of.

The Zodiac War

David stared off into a sparse expanse in the night sky. Julia sat with her brother at a café table.

She was looking at him. The man was so wispy that a strong beam of starlight might be enough evaporate him. Then they were looking around for any sign of the end times.

A moment of silence in their conversation was enough time to slip back into the vacuum of rumination.

Central to their mother's worldview was an inextinguishable obsession with the stars. Even into her later years, as cancer steadily wracked her aging body, Jasmine's detractors, meaning every rational person, secretly admired her conviction to total lunacy. Her delusions foretold of a preordained conflict between humanity and invaders from the night sky. Jasmine called it The Zodiac War.

For anyone outside of the family, this concept is difficult to explain and even more difficult to believe in. Regardless, David and Julia's mother saw herself as the prophet foreseeing a war against the very constellations.

At the time of her passing, she left behind two children who were the sole inheritors of her weird visions. Truth be told, they wanted nothing to do with what amounted to well diagnosed hallucinations.

That last night, in the serenity of the August evening, Julia's mother looked up at the fleeting Milky Way from her wheelchair and witnessed a lull at the borderline between the stars and light pollution.

"Electric light is humanity's attempt to betray the covenant between night and day." Jasmine said.

This was one maxim of her vision.

As she took her final breaths, Jasmine pulled her daughter close to her chest and reminded Julia how in Islamic eschatology, a sign of the last days would be seen in the rising of the sun in the western horizon. In the end times, Jasmine's prophecy stated that mankind would perform war on the stars, and eventually would reap the consequences in one form or another.

Julia held every reason to disregard her mother's apocalyptic claims, but something clung to the air around the terrible suspicion that her mother was telling the truth. She could tell her mother was not lying when she'd come back from a shrieking possession with dementedly assured knowledge retrieved from another state of mind.

Often times she wondered, "What if it was the case that soon the stars would avenge themselves?"

David thought it was another way of saying, "What if she was not completely insane?"

In the solemn square, the pair sat at their table beneath a mounted umbrella. Julia watched David mash his peas and scrape salad leaves around his bowl and fill his glass to overflowing drunkenness. She watched him slide an uncorked bottle across the wicker table towards herself.

He didn't really eat. David was too nauseous from the din of voices congealing in the humid summer air going stale with conversation. David saw one waiter sweat into someone's meal. It disgusted him.

Half-jokingly she said, "I have to be honest I can't say you conform to your namesake."

She was trying to get a rise out of him. He didn't respond.

David didn't have the energy. His flesh couldn't bother to grip to its own skeleton. His body was glabrous and bruised along his flabby arms. David's skin was dotted by internal bleeding; and because he was made out of papier-mâché his whole life was constantly burdened by potentially fatal fissures. It was as if his bones were thorny and constantly pricking his muscles and skin from the inside out.

Julia chalked it up to fate.

As they sat quietly, David's hands went shaking towards a red wine glass causing it to spill onto his white shirt revealing a plunging deformity in his chest. It was a hand sized excavation. He still said nothing to his sister. All the while he watched the bayside out of his dark sockets.

It was in moments of embarrassment like these when David didn't like to believe God crafted him; or to think God stabbed his thumbs into the chests of one of his creations, then set cruelties to bake half-way in the heaven-fired kilns of the firmament. Still, hemophilia gave him a sheltered, princely quality.

Julia held her brother's left hand while she dabbed his clothes with a wet rag fetched by a waiter.

After pouring the last of the bottle into his glass, he tried to calm himself down, sending frustration downstream to dilute fresh memories into a stream of consciousness.

"I wanna go home."

The sun fueled by saffron on fire in the east about burnt itself out.

"Don't you wanna help clean out mom's apartment?" She asked.

"No, I don't feel very good. Besides you'd know what I'd keep and what I'd toss."

David was already nervous. He didn't want to look like he thought about it too hard. They buried her seven days ago.

Before heading back home he looked up at the sky and stared into the nearly fully obliterated constellations making their slight appearances. In the decimated patterns charted by astronomers from a previous age, he saw waning matrices carved into of the Milky Way like pictograms on a black bas relief where humanity wrote its first myths.

Above Norfolk, Canis Major, fearful in its depths, cowered like a freshly spayed dog. In the skies over large cities, one can safely assume that Orion had all but retreated into timeless oblivion, leaving behind his belt as a war trophy.

"Maybe Mom was right, I can't tell you why but I feel it. There's something up there. We can't see it and I'm not sure if it's hiding, or if we're the ones hiding, or for that matter if anything is being hidden. But I can feel it."

With that, David dropped a twenty and stood up.

"You can always clean that place out another day." He said.

"I'd prefer to get started tonight."

"Okay."

"Night Julie, I love you."

"Love you too."

She looked down the cobbled street and watched her brother limp away like a drunken marionette. As David walked, she spotted a light passing just above his head where the constellation Orion aimed a shooting star towards earth's atmosphere. It was abnormally bright.

The wayward ice ball gathered everyone's attention. In the square pedestrians took snapshots. Parents pointed upwards at the comet's night-blue tail to show their children some splendor. It shambled with the speed of highly meticulous lightning.

Julia's heart held agrip, then beat triplets.

The comet slashed slowly, then more precisely, hurtling overhead like a skipping diamond cast into a dark sea. Its speed brought with it an awesome hush capable of stuttering dinner conversations to whispers.

At first Julia was walking slowly down the street towards her mom's house. She increased her pace. Then she realized she forgot to pay, and felt enamored by guilt, but it did not compare to a jumpstart in panicking. She looked overhead. The comet followed her, leaving behind its vibrant ashes as evidence of self-cremation. Patrons of restaurants and busboys and bums begging collided their vision in unanimous awe. It was not just one, but an oncoming meteor shower.

Twenty minutes or so passed before Julia reached the bounds of a gateway in front of her mother's home. The sky flickering in glassine color caught the attention of even more spectators down the road. She unlocked the gate and looked at her mother's unkempt garden. As the comet got closer it began to hiss red from the western sky.

Anxiously, the young woman began tending to her mother's plants where diseased jade clamored amongst a cornucopia of declining ferns. Lopsided succulents drying out in lotus-like patterns sat court attendant to a beheaded dahlia. A jade plant's dehydrated tendrils became weak to the touch, then anti-foliate, then nude. She did what she could with fresh water and soil and went inside.

She thought, "On the walls were our childhood drawings, pictures of us, pictures of dad and mom standing in our old front yard. It smelled like her food, and the candles she liked. Inside was every indicator of motherly comforts but there was no mother. There on the ground by her sofa sat an unfinished sweater pricked by knitting needles and yarn. I had the instinct to finish it, had I remembered the patterns. Or I'd cook her recipes using her spices, had I the time to learn.

On the kitchen table there was an unopened college acceptance letter. I got the email and was gonna tell her I got in. When I was going through our old scrap books I was stunned by the sublimity of coincidence. There in her exhausted arms, in the hospital bed, a newborn baby laid on her mother's chest. It was me. Right next to our first photo together there was picture of my old cat taken after he was born, no larger than my finger's breadth curling darkly into his mother's white bosom.

All I want is for her to see what my children look like."

As Julia set some tea for herself, an intense blue came in from the window and embroidered itself on the living room floor through the lace curtains.

Julia peeked her head through the blinds. A rapturous shockwave caused wind to pulse back into her lungs.

The once vibrant din of dreamlike café dwellers and window shoppers were halted into an astonishment of heart. The stars themselves appeared to fall, and the abysmal sky transformed into bright horror as a meteor erupted loudly pronouncing destruction's one thousand names, written in a glittering comet tail script overhead.

Down the riverside and out into the bay, the whole coastline was subsumed under a field of falling canola flowers. She was hypnotized and went out to see the mesmerizing rain falling as stars. Out in the street to the right and left people were looking up at a miracle.

A sudden thumping began on her mother's neighbor's roof, and the eaves next door, and then on all eaves at once.

A hailstorm bequeathing crystals poured onto the street sides and upon the people watching the meteor shower. Then a teenage boy went down. Screaming started. Julia ran panicking and huddled towards her mother's driveway. She hid beneath a mini-van while the world ended.

Lapis lazuli prized since antiquity burst onto the sidewalk. Julia closed her eyes, hiding from the ice cube sized hailstones hissing out of Jannah. The comet itself, exploding out of space dispersed a punishing rain in brilliant blues, in topaz, in aquamarine all terrible to behold.

Galloping hail battered restaurant goers, who only moments earlier, were content to simply glare at benign beauty. A beauty which rendered itself fatal, like immolate fireworks blossoming overhead then refusing to extinguish as they met the ground.

As the drumming hail continued, she opened her eyes to find herself still alive. Hiding beneath the car, Julia saw flickering neon signs completely bashed out, heads advertising opened brains, and pale limbs mashed by the comet's cruelty.

Glassy storefront windows had burst onto a proudly dressed old woman. Julia saw from underneath the van bumper that the old woman was slumped over, sitting like an unconscious drunk in the middle of the road. Her white dress drowned red; a wrinkled body pounded by an ambuscade of pearls.

Julia curled up, hiding from ice pattering snares on the metal car hood hiding her head.

Heaven melted. The sky's borders collapsed inwards. It was as if the dimensions of Pure Land Buddhism or Islam's Garden collided with a small bayside resort city caught utterly unprepared.

Some minutes passed. After realizing the storm had ended Julia limped out from under the safety of the totaled vehicle.

She looked around the street corners and saw bodies in human piles strewn down a city block. The swordlike comet sheathed itself in the cosmos. She limped out of her mother's terrace and saw a dead dog.

In fact she saw many dead dogs laying besides their many owners. If you had just blown into town from anywhere in the world or had recently woken up, having slept through the apocalypse, you could rightfully assume that this 21st century town had been raided by a horde of ghosts. Ice balls mixed with meteorite laid around destroyed avenues. Windshields were webbed into broken patterns, and glass shards were flung everywhere, not withholding skin.

Julia was walking in a daze.

Eventually, she stumbled towards a man she recognized. It was her brother. His shirt was torn, exposing that plunging crevasse in his chest. A point of shame now a comparably pointless mark of vanity. David was laid out, battered to mincemeat, with a fist sized diamond embedded in his chest.

To her surprise he opened his eyes. Survivors who did not perish groaned. Others, more able bodied, tended to their loved ones and friends and complete strangers. A single doctor found himself helpless to every degree, responding to dizzying calls for an army of ambulances.

She sat on the pavement holding her brother. Though he managed a stuttering of syllables in her ears. Julia watched David wheeze in a lisp.

His blood wasn't clotting. It ran down his nose in twin streams pooling in his mouth.

She held him all night, looking together for the rising sun, seeking warmth for his cool skin. And in spite of shock David grinned upwards at the constellations clinging to their nightly empire. He went unconscious but his heart was still beating. She laid by him.

His blood reflected the deaths of stars, then their rebirth in the scarlet of heavens held high.

Key Bardo

In the late afternoon, a pliant fiberglass boat of 56 yards length could transport passengers directly from Marco Island to the Florida Keys. To Michael and Naomi, 50 dollars and 6 hours is a fair exchange in place of a long drive across the peninsula.

During the summer months the Everglades become all encompassingly lush and the mangrove swamps are infested with every type of cold blooded shadow South Florida could offer.

Looking over the boat's port side Michael watched the florid coastline. In his mind the mangroves embodied its green and brown inhabitants, living in their slithering labyrinth.

"Trust me honey a boat ride is simply more efficient."

She nodded. He kept watch on jungle feeding upon itself.

"There it goes." He said.

Each wave they surmounted was a therapeutic relief to him.

Naomi turned to her husband.

"I know you don't like to drive anymore. But I could have done all the driving and you could've just relaxed."

"I know but this way is cheaper if you think about it. Besides in July there's a higher risk of wildfire."

"You gotta get back into a car one of these days."

He kept silent.

"Maybe on our way back from Key West we could rent one? Something cool?" She asked.

"We'll have to see."

Naomi felt her question quickly smothered under the weight of possibility. Perhaps it was the Caribbean sun beating down on her. Michael kept looking overboard. After sitting together in the sweltering sun for ten minutes she went back inside the ship's cabin to read her book.

Closing his eyes in the coarse refreshment of possibility, a steady misting of sea water salted his lips. Thinking again of the Everglades, he checked the horizon behind him to make sure the Mexican Gulf looked limitless.

Taking to wet concentration, the sea was verdant with its own hidden glades. The sargasso shadows ambled upwards, decaying at roots of resounding depth. Rarely did any seaweed come to the top. He closed his eyes and fell asleep in place as if earthly locations floated from over the horizon towards a stand still vessel.

Waking up to darkness, the boat floated into the docking cove. Key West had arrived.

"Wake up." Naomi whispered. "Look we're here."

After a happy dream Michael found himself completely covered from head to toe in salt. Every surface of skin on his body was dusted in ashen particles.

Looking drowsily into the blackness of the waves, a noir mirror formed on a sable sky in the rippling water, revealing a certain blackness of the mind. The stars in that floating endless mind came to their crests on blinking wave caps.

He looked towards the island.

There were the ship beacons, red stars, the cove reflecting pathways to shore-bound homes aglow. He was sinking downwards. Then rising. Floating. Then falling. Naomi shook him. He leapt awake panicking.

Michael was a pillar of salt from hours of windy wash but Naomi's squinting eyes provided an escape route to tranquility; likewise an escape route to pleasure that is always luminously clear. Key West.

The sound of waves ebbed into the next morning.

A copy of Kawabata's *Snow Country* was laying on the bedside table. Flipping over to look at the other side of the hotel room, Michael watched his wife step out of the shower. Her cotton robe slipped over her curvatures, draping artfully as she traipsed out onto the balcony to face the Caribbean. She was calm. Calm enough to be thought of sexually without guilt. He got out of bed and made a pot of coffee.

At the cusp of her updo, Michael pressed his lips against nape of Naomi's neck, wrapping his arms tenderly around her body. A hot mug went into her hands.

He knew there was plenty to get into during the evening. There were bars, restaurants. There were other sorts of risqué places.

In fact Key West is a convex of pleasures. You could even imagine that it is too warm for there to be a morgue so nothing needs to die.

Chickens peck at food left behind by restaurants or at mosquitoes, but the mosquitoes are unanimously declared to be undead. The roosters and hens that throng the island perform a public service so they are not killed. From the back end of his mind Michael knew that in Key West there is nothing to do with death, so it must be imported.

The sea view was mesmerizing; how the sea washes water so perfectly that every wave is made to look like it's been following instructions to churn for an eternity. If anything comes to pass, the waves will wash it away and make it like the rest of sea.

"We should go to the beach tonight. It's absolutely clear. There's not even a single jellyfish on the shore." Michael said.

"Then we must be very far from New Jersey."

"You know down the street there's a nice breakfast place. We should get something to eat before we start our day. I'm hungry for eggs."

"Eggs make me queasy. I was already sick this morning and I don't think I'm in the mood. You go. I'll meet you in an hour." She said. "Also one more thing Michael, please don't flush condoms, it clogs the drain."

"Did you throw them away?" Michael asked.

"I'm not sticking my hand in there! You do it!" Naomi said half laughing, half repulsed.

"Fine, I'll get them." He sighed. "I'll see you later, just call me when you're on your way."

Before going out Michael went to the toilet. Floating flaccid with slime, a translucent relic of sexual liberty got flung into the trash. He took some honest pleasure in last night's reminder. It was a beautiful sterile love breached at closest contact between two bellies, with nothing but a latex wall to separate them. One stomach freshly taught, woven with stretch marks, and another pregnant only with luxury. Suddenly they had a lot of money and nobody in particular to spend it on.

Michael's attendance to danger had dissipated back into youth's unlucky invincibility. 26 is young for almost fatherhood. Deciding consciously that the deceptively long streets were worth but a glance, his sandals went down the hotel porch steps, flopping carelessly across the road.

Michael, never being very careful, did not look both ways.

Whitehead Street was home to the highest point on the island where a lighthouse is situated across the street from Hemingway's home. The next highest point is a banyan tree, all of which Naomi intended to see today. Walking down the sidewalk the banyan's boughs, like the mangroves, glittered green.

Its branches supplicate in many directions all stemming from the same trunk. Similarly to lives, some stretch out and interweave, some return to the ground as quickly as conceived.

Naomi, longstanding on the balcony, stared silently, inconsolable. Thinking of tender baby noises, down on the sidewalk a chick's shrill freshness softened her. There was that irreconcilable softness lost to her in the material world. In dreams she has the sensory-memory of her child's toes.

 Never hesitating to smile at any baby, she savored in any opportunity to lavish in what young parents roll their eyes at. As an aunt she wasn't even phased by vomit or diapers. Changing a baby's diaper was an act of love. For the brief 13 months they were alive together, her child taught her the maternal compassion of responsibility. In pregnancy, she was breathing for her baby and eating for her baby. No action was vicarious. Anymore sensitive and she would've been entirely overwhelmed by all minutiae.

There is that particular way a person can remain staring at any of the world's goings on and steadily space out. The mind's eye, or a memory, or a dream, can hallucinate old images before your eyes in broad daylight. Before you know it, you're staring directly into the past.

At the shore in Naples, Naomi's request was that the seafloor accepts her son's bones.

Naomi wept in pangs, clutching her roots of red hair. Then asking hallucinatory questions.

"Where is my boy?"

"We gave him back." He told her.

"To who?"

"To God."

"We gotta go get him."

"God has him now." Michael repeated, pulling her close.

As the last atoms of the boy dispersed, feeding into the endless chain, Naomi's father read from *The Tibetan Book of the Dead*. How strange it is that our brain takes a registry of memories, even of hysterical hallucinations.

"Oh child of noble family, it's time for the Bardo Thodol to enter your consciousness."

Terror stricken, Michael began to wonder how many times this was recited.

"But where is..."

An imam from the local mosque in also read Surah Ya-Sin just to be safe, even though he protested the boy's cremation.

He reminded the attendees in a gruff tone, "In Islam you are strictly prohibited from burning remains and they must be buried."

A shard of heat lightning cut through the sky flinging her out of memory.

Naomi went downstairs to find her husband. She was going to tell him that she would be driving back home alone.

At the café, Michael overheard a man discussing a vasectomy with his wife. "It's amazing what clinical technology will permit these days."

On his own Michael had briefly considered it. He imagined the crude joy of fucking forever without the fear of impregnation. His eggs came out over fried. The nauseating bile of jealousy burned the back of Michael's mouth. He salved his burns with swallows of orange juice.

Yes it was a nice thought.

He had tried his hand at child rearing. It was easier thinking about it as a post-natal abortion.

"The Spartans left their's to die on Greek mountain sides." He muttered to himself. The thoughts were intrusive.

Was it embarrassing to be relinquished from such a responsibility? Some souls feel an overwhelming urge to return to from whence they came. Not Michael. He wanted to live as long as he could. Which means hopefully forever.

In three handfuls Michael remembered how she let the ashes fly, once for creation, once for destruction, and once for resurrection. Honestly he could scarcely recall such an embarrassing level of freedom.

As the last physical evidence of the boy flushed inwards and outwards on the shore, he could envision the whole scene submersed in birdsong.

Michael started thinking for himself.

"For a second I thought that I would never die. Coincidentally, my cousin Eddie quoted the Bible during his eulogy."

How strange it is that our brain takes a registry of the memory of thought, even of intrusive thought.

Eddie read, "And the Lord said, 'Be not over much wicked, neither be thou foolish: why shouldest thou die before thy time?"

"At the funeral the saffron sun began to emerge in garish luminosity. While shining upon my face it made me think to myself: I am still here.

I couldn't speak frankly with the family and friends who had made it down to Naples for the funeral. In fact it was evidence of the failure of words, a failure of sensation too.

What did lunch taste like that day? Only the flavor of grief burning time as residual air. I was sure a lot of nice things were said about him, my boy. Was I sad? Yes. Did I hear the speeches of those elderly speaking abstractly of death? What right do they have? They've already had their shot. At the end of the day I'm going to be filtered through the mangrove too, or the banyan's veins, or into seaweed. I refuse to spend any more time on these thoughts. I will be happy at any costs. If I am hated for it, very well then."

He remembered that he remembered that he did not want to remember, nor did he even want to be conscious of memory.

How strange it is that our brain takes a registry of… He saw Naomi come walking down the sidewalk looking like the girl from Ipanema. He waved and smiled, but she just doesn't see.

Acknowledgements

I would like to thank the good people at *Fugitives and Futurists*, *Apocalypse Confidential*, and *ExPat Press* for publishing my work. Thank you to my dear friend and first reader George Balchunas for his persistent advice throughout the years. Also, to my loving family, always.